RED ONE™

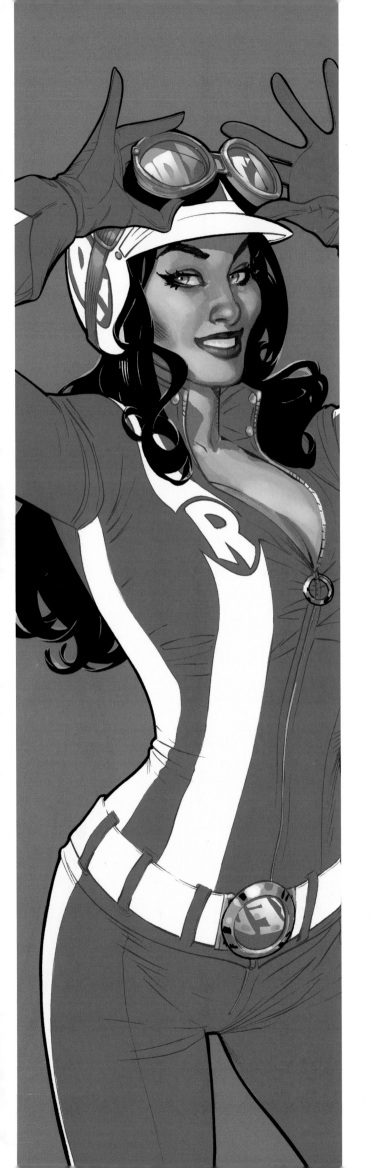

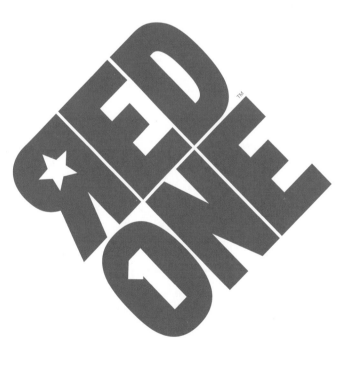

UNDERCOVER
BOOK 2

UNDERCOVER BOOK 2

CREATED BY
XAVIER DORISON
& TERRY DODSON

XAVIER DORISON
SCRIPT

WITH THE COLLABORATION OF
ANTOINE CRISTAU

TERRY DODSON
PENCILS & COLORS

RACHEL DODSON
INKS

CLAYTON COWLES
LETTERS

**FANNY HURTEL &
TERRY DODSON**
TRANSLATORS

GILLIAN RENK
FLATS

**PHILIPPE HAURI &
LAUREN SANKOVITCH**
EDITORS

RED ONE UNDERCOVER BOOK TWO HC. ISBN: 978-1-63215-935-9. First Printing. January 2017. Published by Image Comics, Inc. Office of publication: 2701 NW Vaughn St., Ste. 780, Portland, OR 97210. Copyright © 2017
Xavier Dorison & Terry Dodson. All rights reserved. Originally published in single magazine form as RED ONE #3-4. RED ONE™ (including all prominent characters featured herein), its logo and all character likenesses
are trademarks of Xavier Dorison & Terry Dodson, unless otherwise noted. Image Comics® and its logos are registered trademarks of Image Comics, Inc. No part of this publication may be reproduced or transmitted, in
any form or by any means (except for short excerpts for review purposes) without the express written permission of Image Comics, Inc. All names, characters, events and locales in this publication are entirely fictional. Any
resemblance to actual persons (living or dead), events or places, without satiric intent, is coincidental. Printed in the USA. For International Rights inquiries, contact : foreignlicensing@imagecomics.com

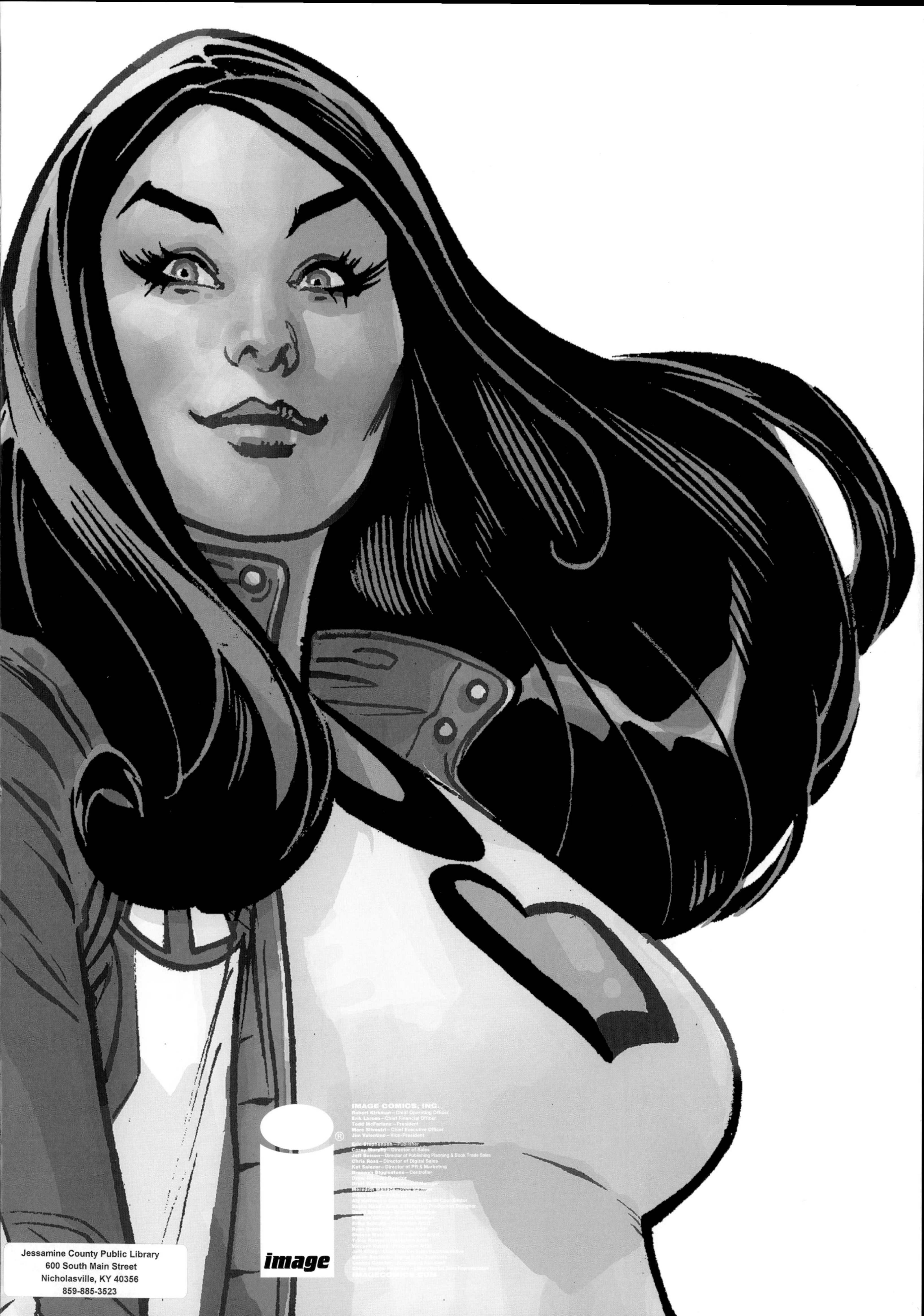
image

IMAGE COMICS, INC.
Robert Kirkman—Chief Operating Officer
Erik Larsen—Chief Financial Officer
Todd McFarlane—President
Marc Silvestri—Chief Executive Officer
Jim Valentino—Vice-President

Eric Stephenson—Publisher
Corey Murphy—Director of Sales
Jeff Boison—Director of Publishing Planning & Book Trade Sales
Chris Ross—Director of Digital Sales
Kat Salazar—Director of PR & Marketing
Branwyn Bigglestone—Controller

красно одно (Red One) was the state function created by Comrade Iosif Vissarionovich Stalin in honor of the female comrades who fell in battle against the tyrannical capitalists during the Great Revolution. Red One is the eternal memory of their bodies, covered in the blood of sacrifice...

...and the last resort for Comrade First Secretary to help the Soviet citizenship in distress.

The year is 1977. Comrade Red One, aka Vera Yelnikov, is dispatched by the Kremlin to Los Angeles to become a superhero and a poster child for Communist propaganda. But when a violent fringe movement emerges and puts her mission in jeopardy, Red One must choose between saving those she's come to care for and her loyalty to the Soviet cause.

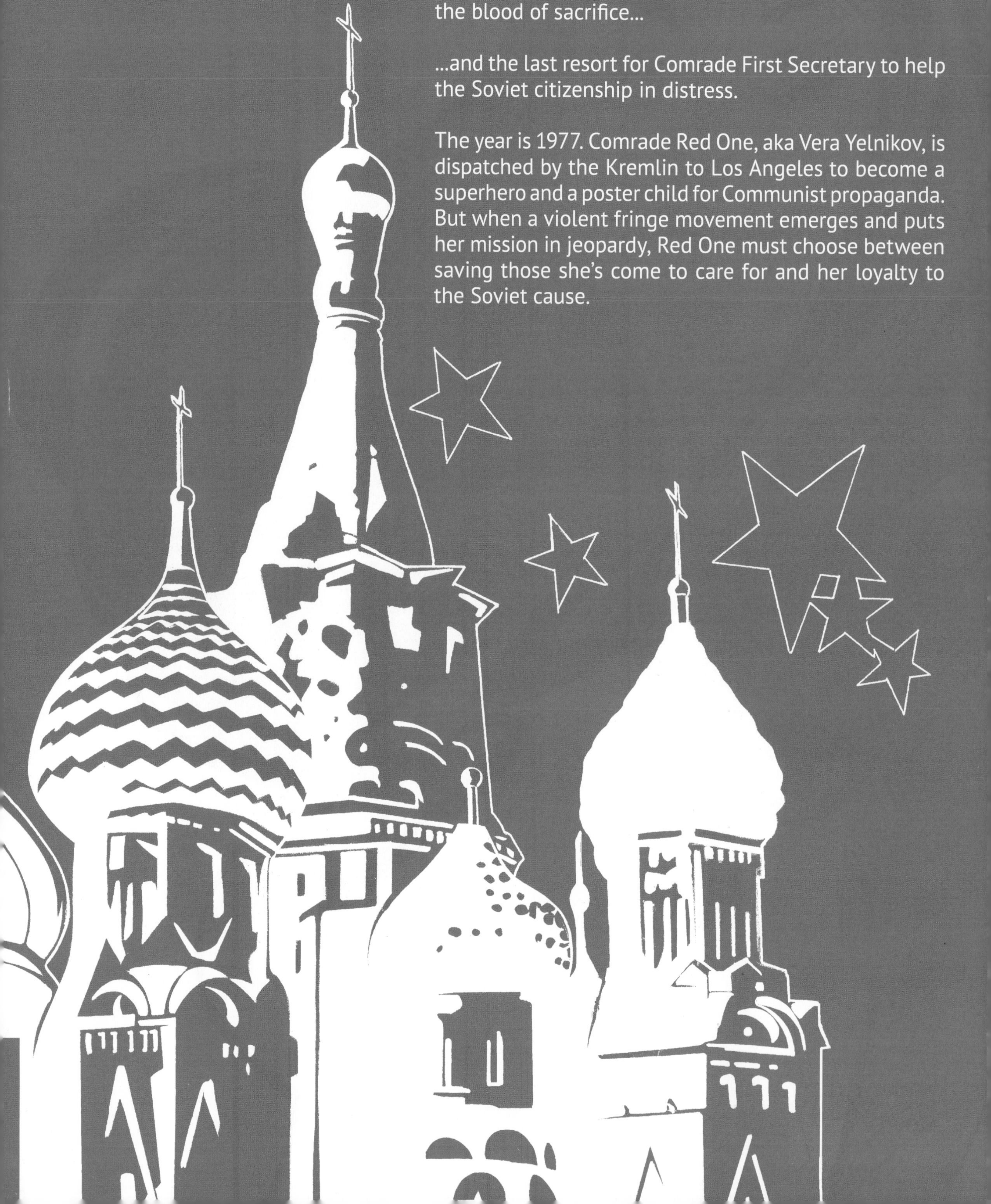

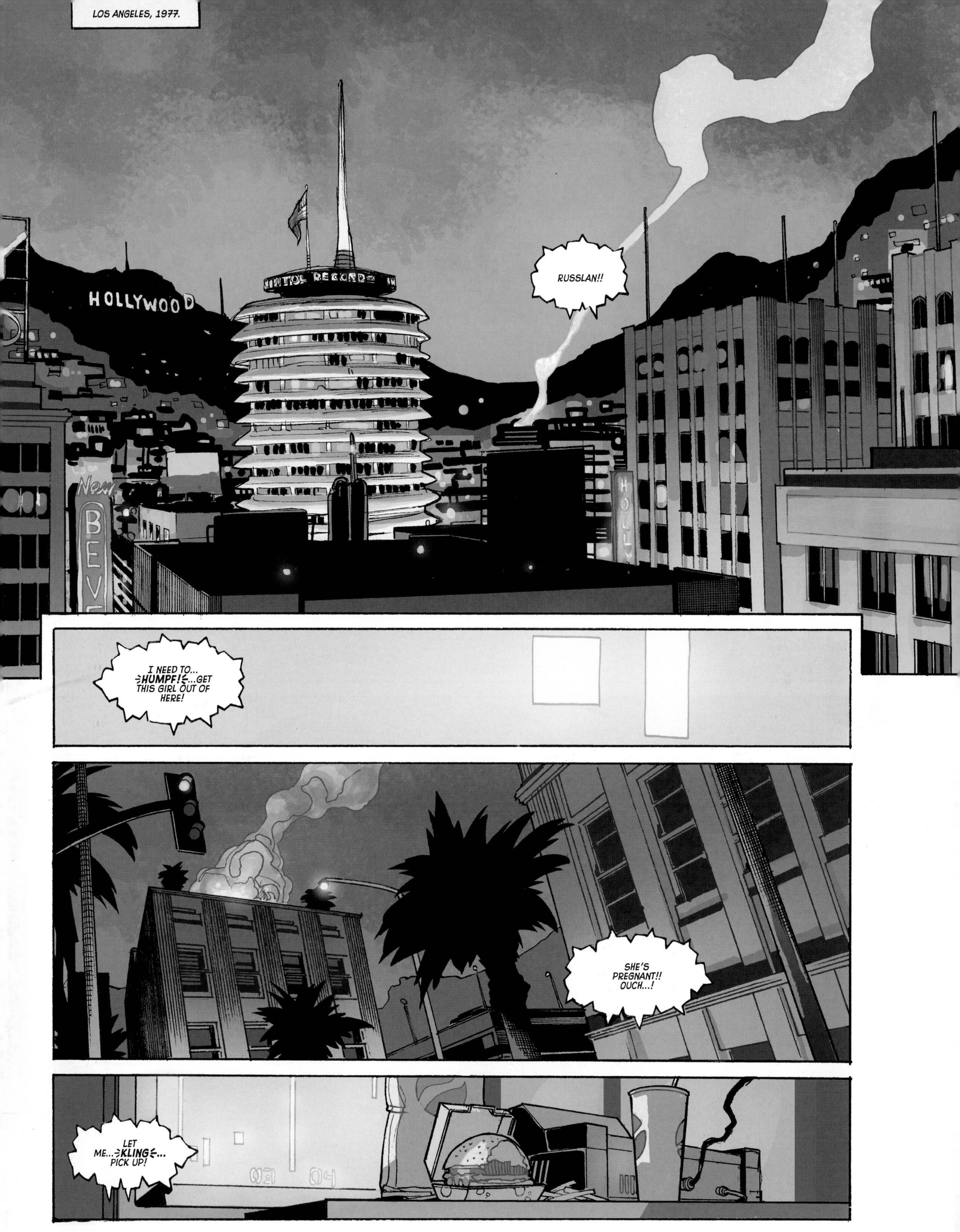
LOS ANGELES, 1977.
HOLLYWOOD
RUSSLAN!!
I NEED TO... HUMPF! ...GET THIS GIRL OUT OF HERE!
SHE'S PREGNANT!! OUCH...!
LET ME... KLING ... PICK UP!

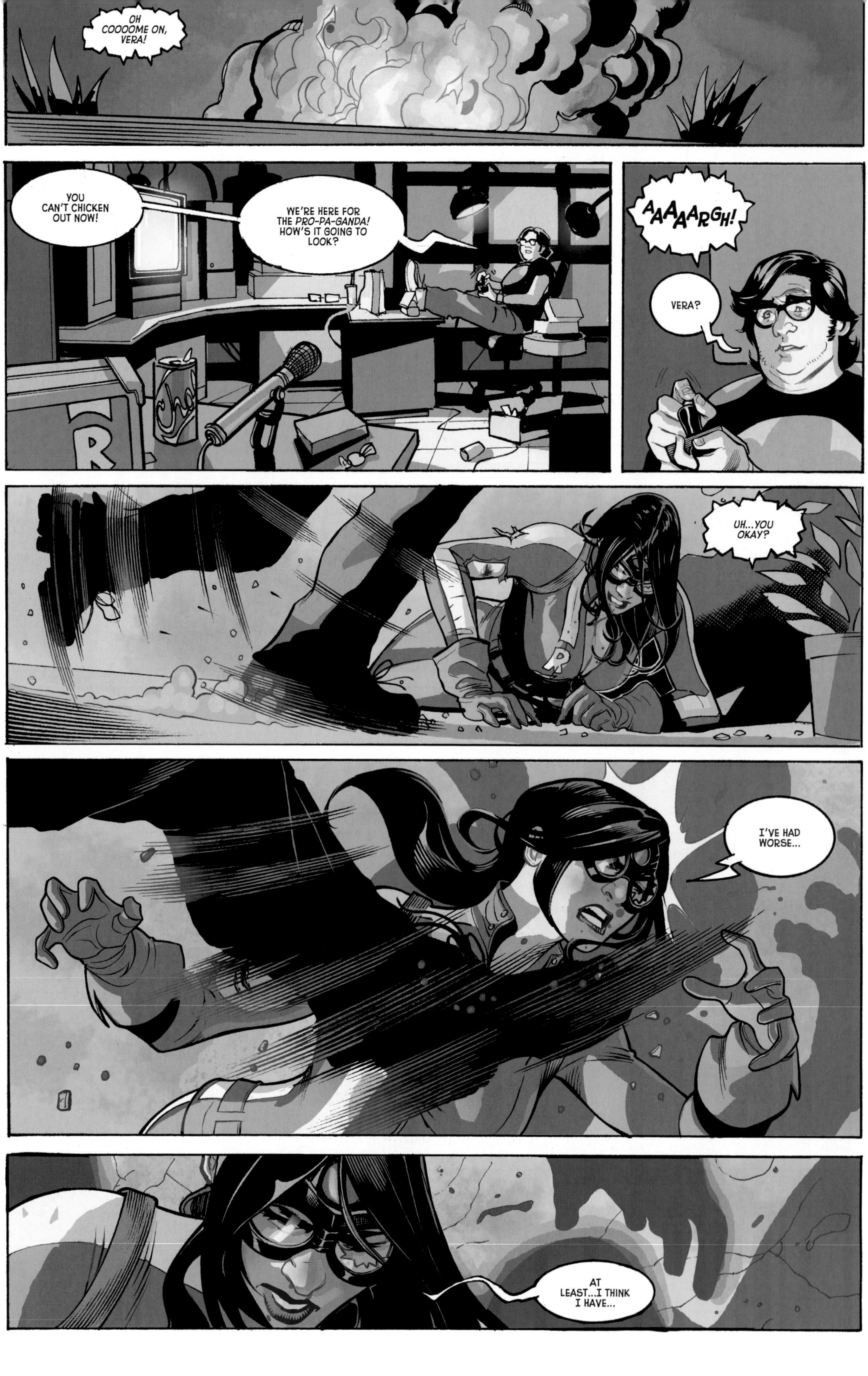
OH COOOOME ON, VERA!
YOU CAN'T CHICKEN OUT NOW!
WE'RE HERE FOR THE PRO-PA-GANDA! HOW'S IT GOING TO LOOK?
AAAAARGH!
VERA?
UH...YOU OKAY?
I'VE HAD WORSE...
AT LEAST...I THINK I HAVE...

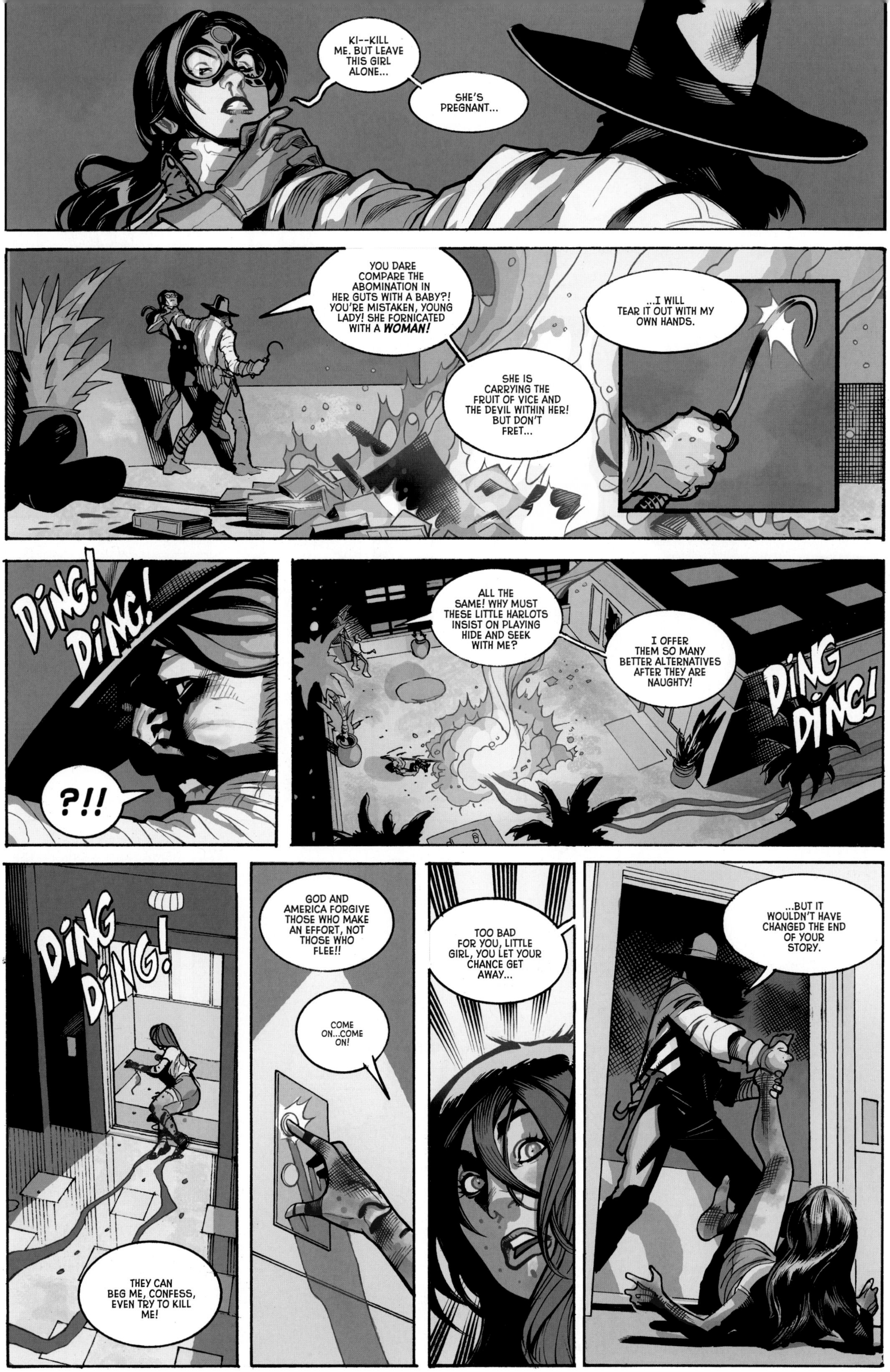
KI--KILL ME. BUT LEAVE THIS GIRL ALONE...
SHE'S PREGNANT...
YOU DARE COMPARE THE ABOMINATION IN HER GUTS WITH A BABY?! YOU'RE MISTAKEN, YOUNG LADY! SHE FORNICATED WITH A WOMAN!
SHE IS CARRYING THE FRUIT OF VICE AND THE DEVIL WITHIN HER! BUT DON'T FRET...
...I WILL TEAR IT OUT WITH MY OWN HANDS.
DING! DING!
?!!
ALL THE SAME! WHY MUST THESE LITTLE HARLOTS INSIST ON PLAYING HIDE AND SEEK WITH ME?
I OFFER THEM SO MANY BETTER ALTERNATIVES AFTER THEY ARE NAUGHTY!
DING DING!
DING DING!
THEY CAN BEG ME, CONFESS, EVEN TRY TO KILL ME!
GOD AND AMERICA FORGIVE THOSE WHO MAKE AN EFFORT, NOT THOSE WHO FLEE!!
COME ON...COME ON!
TOO BAD FOR YOU, LITTLE GIRL, YOU LET YOUR CHANCE GET AWAY...
...BUT IT WOULDN'T HAVE CHANGED THE END OF YOUR STORY.

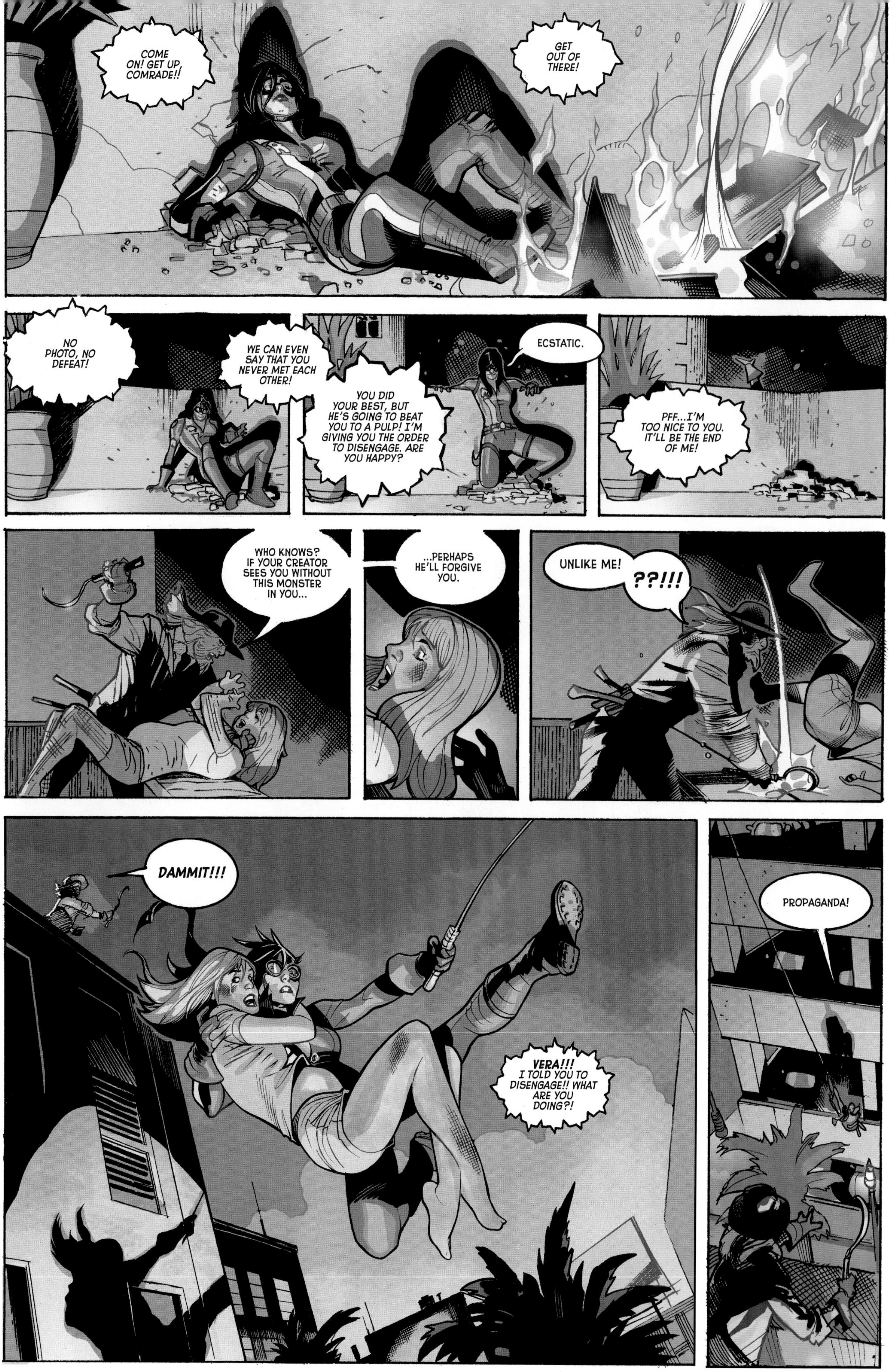
COME ON! GET UP, COMRADE!!
GET OUT OF THERE!
NO PHOTO, NO DEFEAT!
WE CAN EVEN SAY THAT YOU NEVER MET EACH OTHER!
YOU DID YOUR BEST, BUT HE'S GOING TO BEAT YOU TO A PULP! I'M GIVING YOU THE ORDER TO DISENGAGE. ARE YOU HAPPY?
ECSTATIC.
PFF...I'M TOO NICE TO YOU. IT'LL BE THE END OF ME!
WHO KNOWS? IF YOUR CREATOR SEES YOU WITHOUT THIS MONSTER IN YOU...
...PERHAPS HE'LL FORGIVE YOU.
UNLIKE ME!
??!!!
DAMMIT!!!
VERA!!! I TOLD YOU TO DISENGAGE!! WHAT ARE YOU DOING?!
PROPAGANDA!

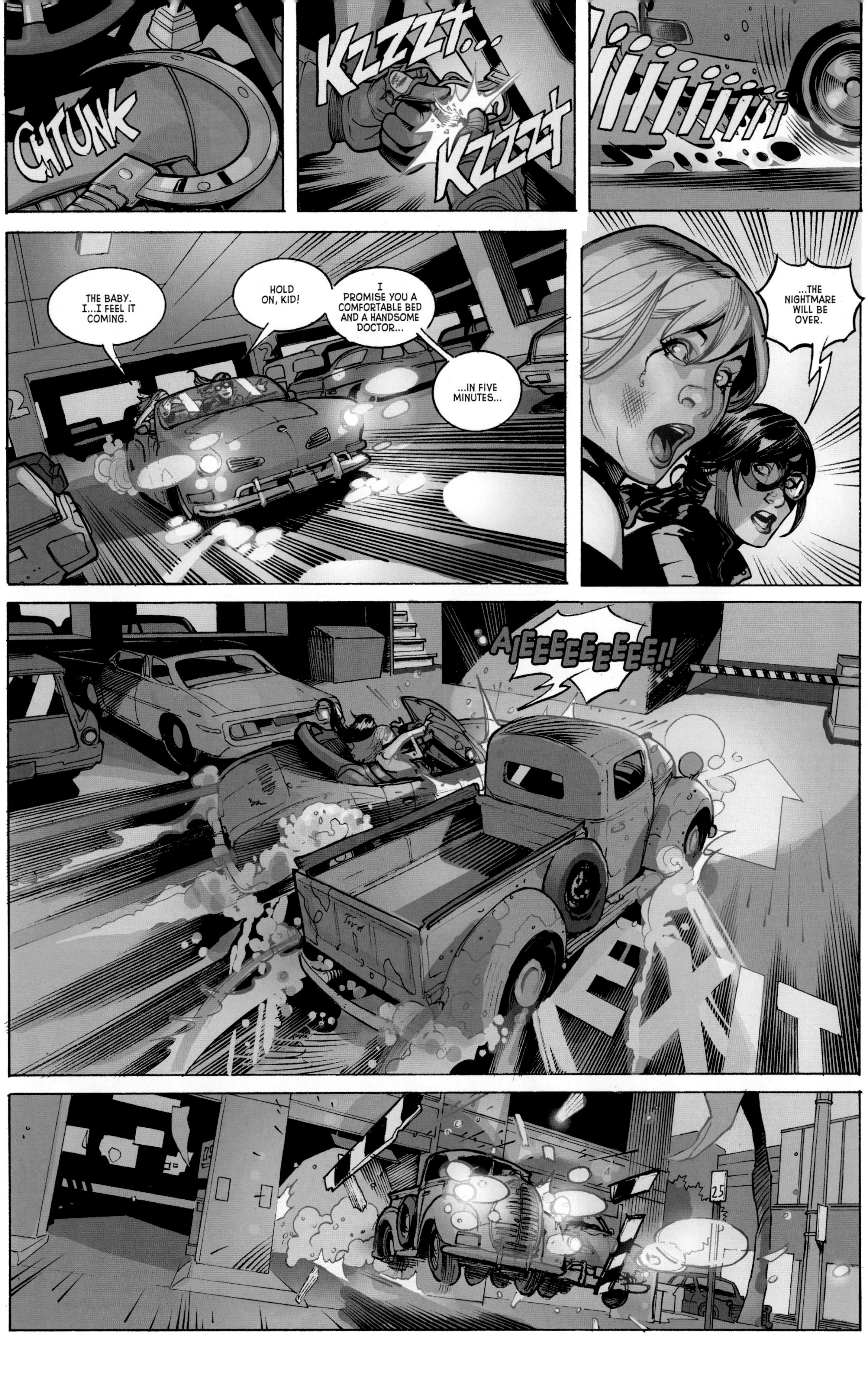
CHTUNK
KZZZT...
KZZZT
IIIIIIIIIII
THE BABY. I...I FEEL IT COMING.
HOLD ON, KID!
I PROMISE YOU A COMFORTABLE BED AND A HANDSOME DOCTOR...
...IN FIVE MINUTES...
...THE NIGHTMARE WILL BE OVER.
AIEEEEEEEEEE!!
EXIT
25

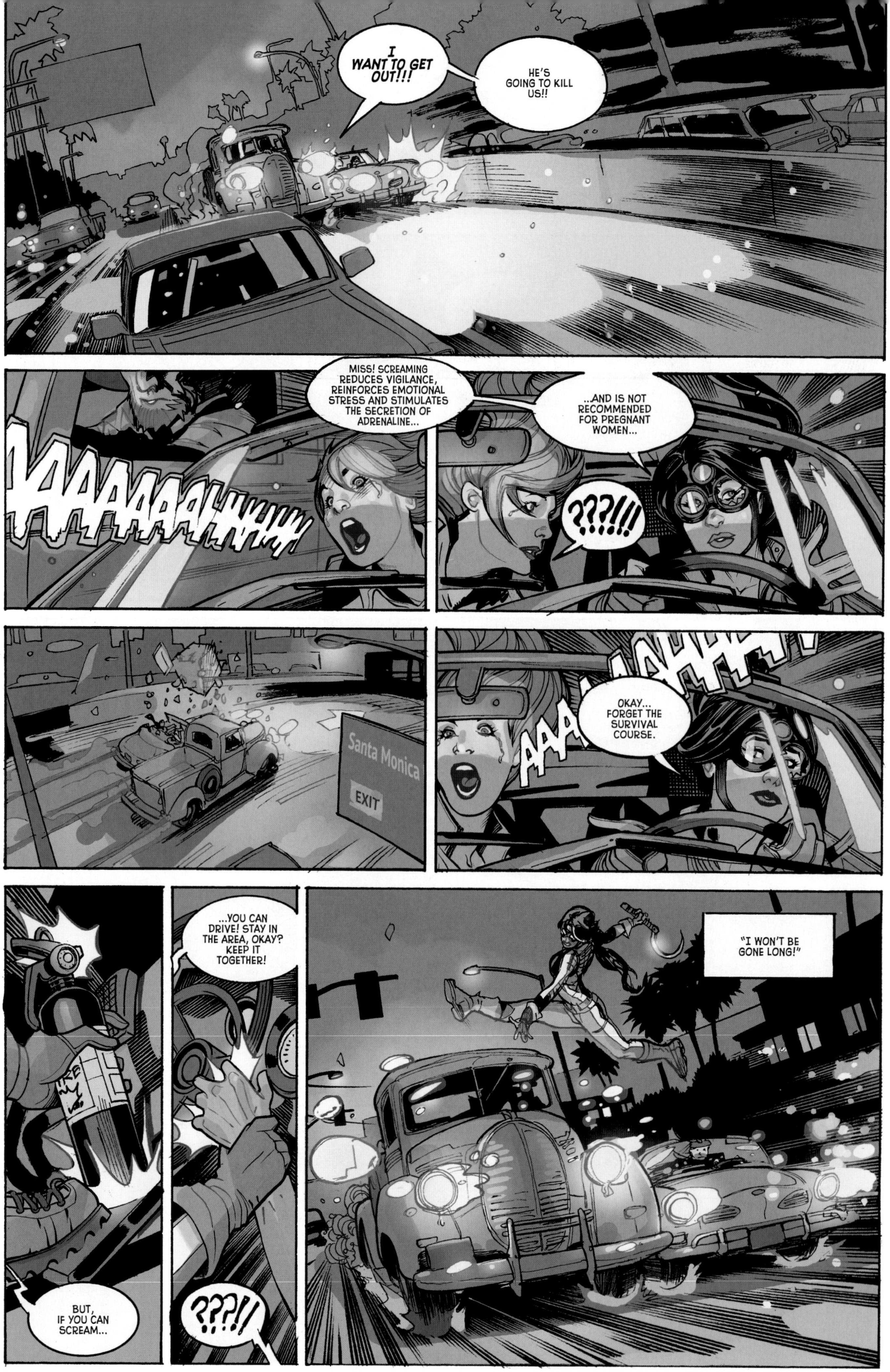
I WANT TO GET OUT!!!
HE'S GOING TO KILL US!!
MISS! SCREAMING REDUCES VIGILANCE, REINFORCES EMOTIONAL STRESS AND STIMULATES THE SECRETION OF ADRENALINE...
AAAAAAAAHHHHH
...AND IS NOT RECOMMENDED FOR PREGNANT WOMEN...
???!!!
Santa Monica
EXIT
OKAY... FORGET THE SURVIVAL COURSE.
BUT, IF YOU CAN SCREAM...
...YOU CAN DRIVE! STAY IN THE AREA, OKAY? KEEP IT TOGETHER!
???!!
"I WON'T BE GONE LONG!"

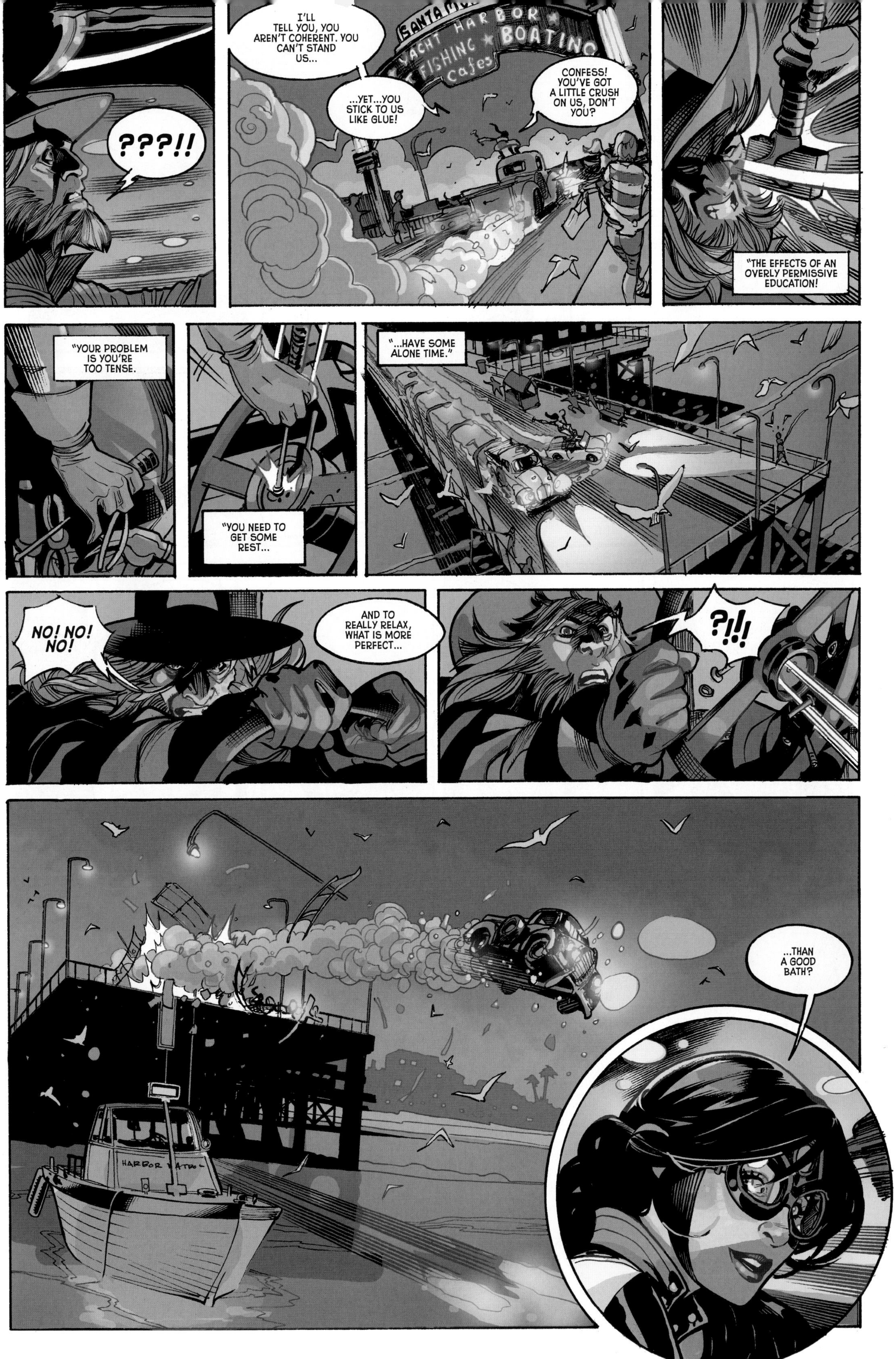
???!!
I'LL TELL YOU, YOU AREN'T COHERENT. YOU CAN'T STAND US...
...YET...YOU STICK TO US LIKE GLUE!
SANTA MO... YACHT HARBOR FISHING BOATING Cafes
CONFESS! YOU'VE GOT A LITTLE CRUSH ON US, DON'T YOU?
"THE EFFECTS OF AN OVERLY PERMISSIVE EDUCATION!
"YOUR PROBLEM IS YOU'RE TOO TENSE.
"YOU NEED TO GET SOME REST...
"...HAVE SOME ALONE TIME."
NO! NO! NO!
AND TO REALLY RELAX, WHAT IS MORE PERFECT...
?!!!
HARBOR PATROL
...THAN A GOOD BATH?

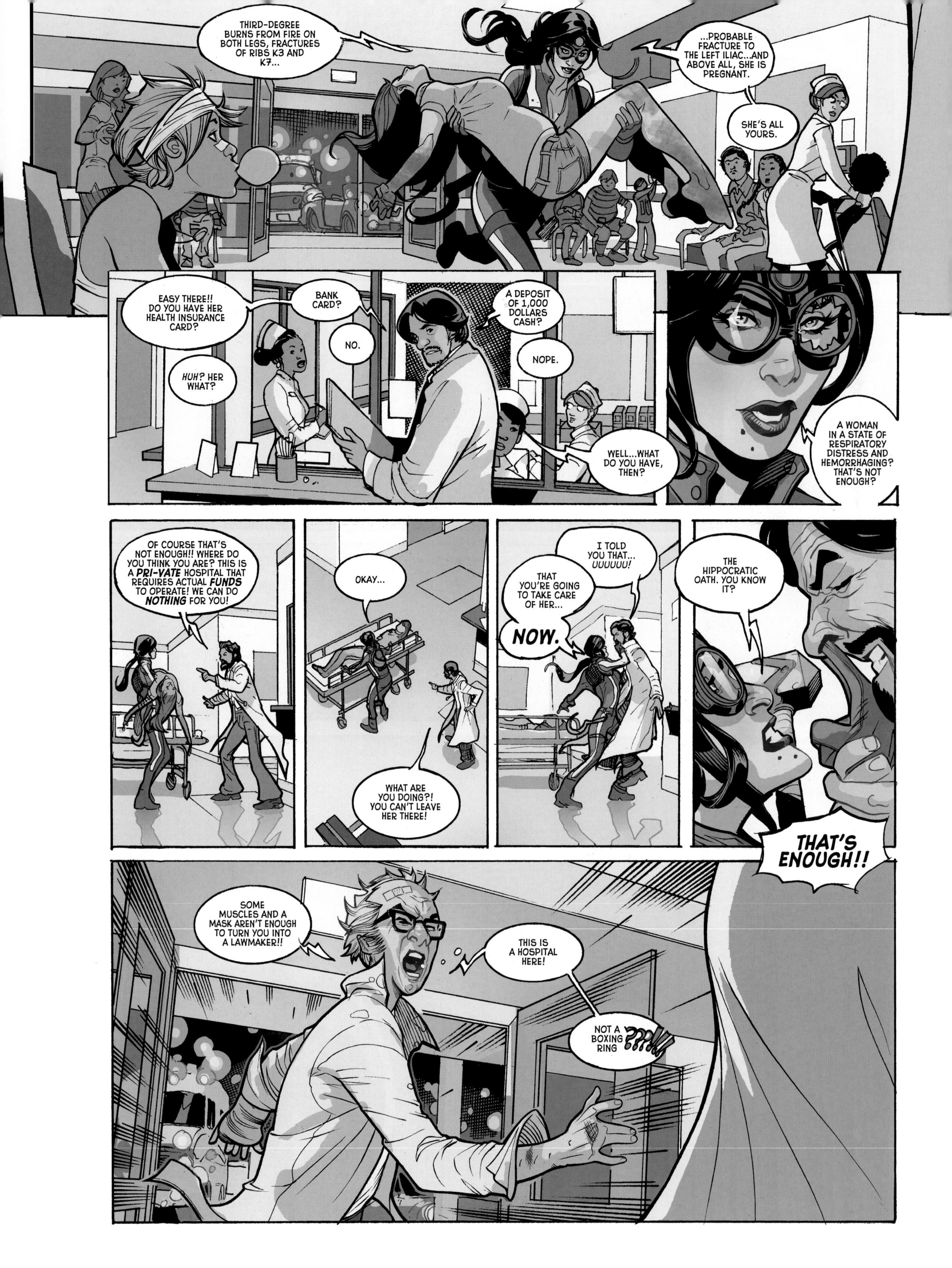
THIRD-DEGREE BURNS FROM FIRE ON BOTH LEGS, FRACTURES OF RIBS K3 AND K7...
...PROBABLE FRACTURE TO THE LEFT ILIAC...AND ABOVE ALL, SHE IS PREGNANT.
SHE'S ALL YOURS.
EASY THERE!! DO YOU HAVE HER HEALTH INSURANCE CARD?
HUH? HER WHAT?
BANK CARD?
NO.
A DEPOSIT OF 1,000 DOLLARS CASH?
NOPE.
WELL...WHAT DO YOU HAVE, THEN?
A WOMAN IN A STATE OF RESPIRATORY DISTRESS AND HEMORRHAGING? THAT'S NOT ENOUGH?
OF COURSE THAT'S NOT ENOUGH!! WHERE DO YOU THINK YOU ARE? THIS IS A PRI-VATE HOSPITAL THAT REQUIRES ACTUAL FUNDS TO OPERATE! WE CAN DO NOTHING FOR YOU!
OKAY...
WHAT ARE YOU DOING?! YOU CAN'T LEAVE HER THERE!
I TOLD YOU THAT... UUUUUU!
THAT YOU'RE GOING TO TAKE CARE OF HER...
NOW.
THE HIPPOCRATIC OATH. YOU KNOW IT?
THAT'S ENOUGH!!
SOME MUSCLES AND A MASK AREN'T ENOUGH TO TURN YOU INTO A LAWMAKER!!
THIS IS A HOSPITAL HERE!
NOT A BOXING RING ???!!

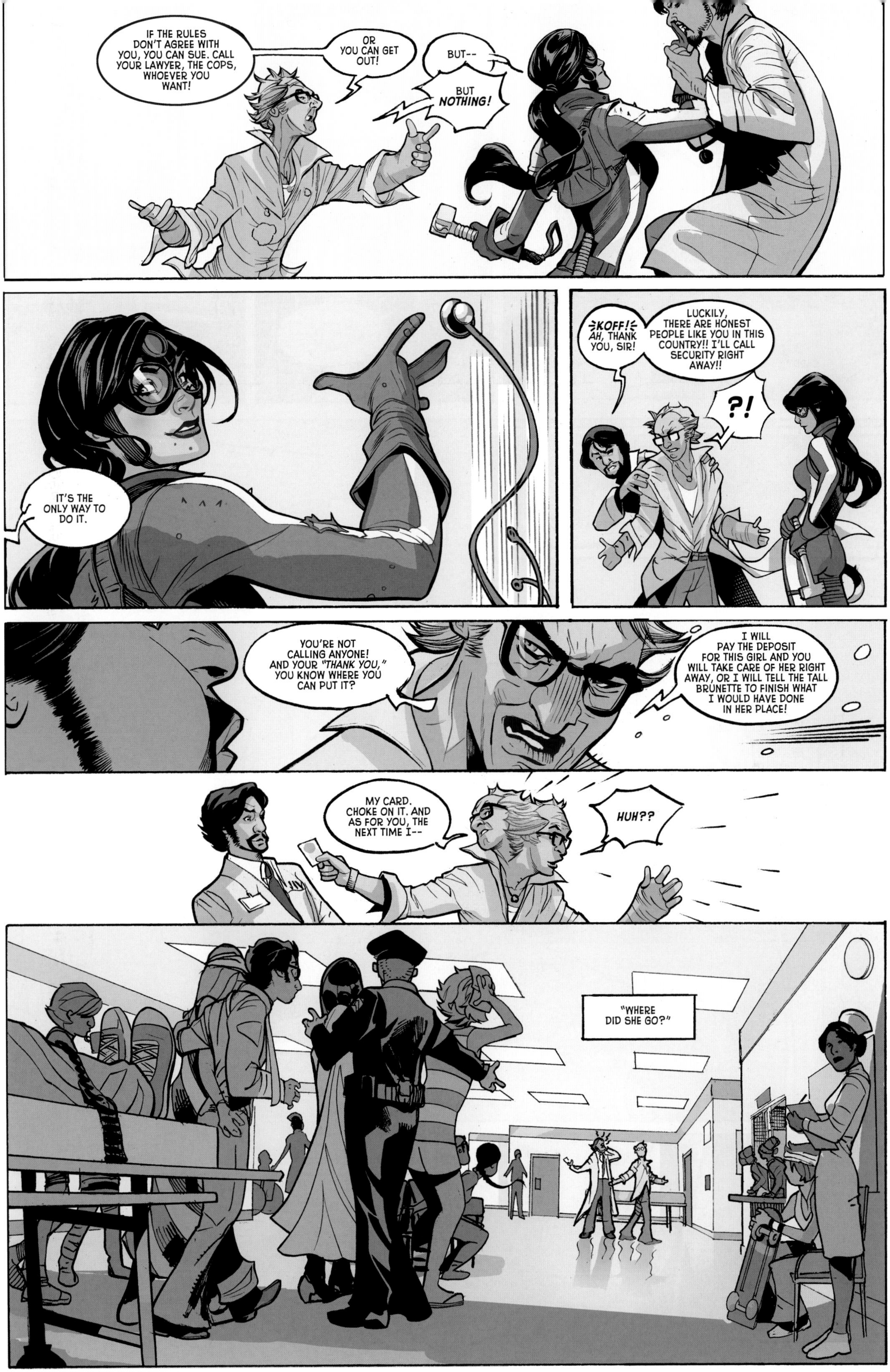
IF THE RULES DON'T AGREE WITH YOU, YOU CAN SUE. CALL YOUR LAWYER, THE COPS, WHOEVER YOU WANT!
OR YOU CAN GET OUT!
BUT--
BUT NOTHING!
IT'S THE ONLY WAY TO DO IT.
KOFF! AH, THANK YOU, SIR!
LUCKILY, THERE ARE HONEST PEOPLE LIKE YOU IN THIS COUNTRY!! I'LL CALL SECURITY RIGHT AWAY!!
?!
YOU'RE NOT CALLING ANYONE! AND YOUR "THANK YOU," YOU KNOW WHERE YOU CAN PUT IT?
I WILL PAY THE DEPOSIT FOR THIS GIRL AND YOU WILL TAKE CARE OF HER RIGHT AWAY, OR I WILL TELL THE TALL BRUNETTE TO FINISH WHAT I WOULD HAVE DONE IN HER PLACE!
MY CARD. CHOKE ON IT. AND AS FOR YOU, THE NEXT TIME I--
HUH??
"WHERE DID SHE GO?"

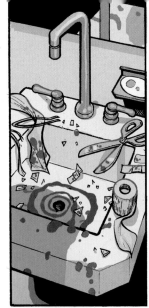

"AT LEAST YOU'RE ALIVE.

HEY YOU! WHY THE LONG FACE?

"YOU'RE IN ONE PIECE.

"YOU HAVE DIMITRI AND MASHA.

"NOT COUNTING THIS LEW AND ALL THE PEOPLE WHO YOU LOVE.

Biiip! Biiip! Biiip!

"AND YOU'RE SMILING!"

THAT'S BETTER!

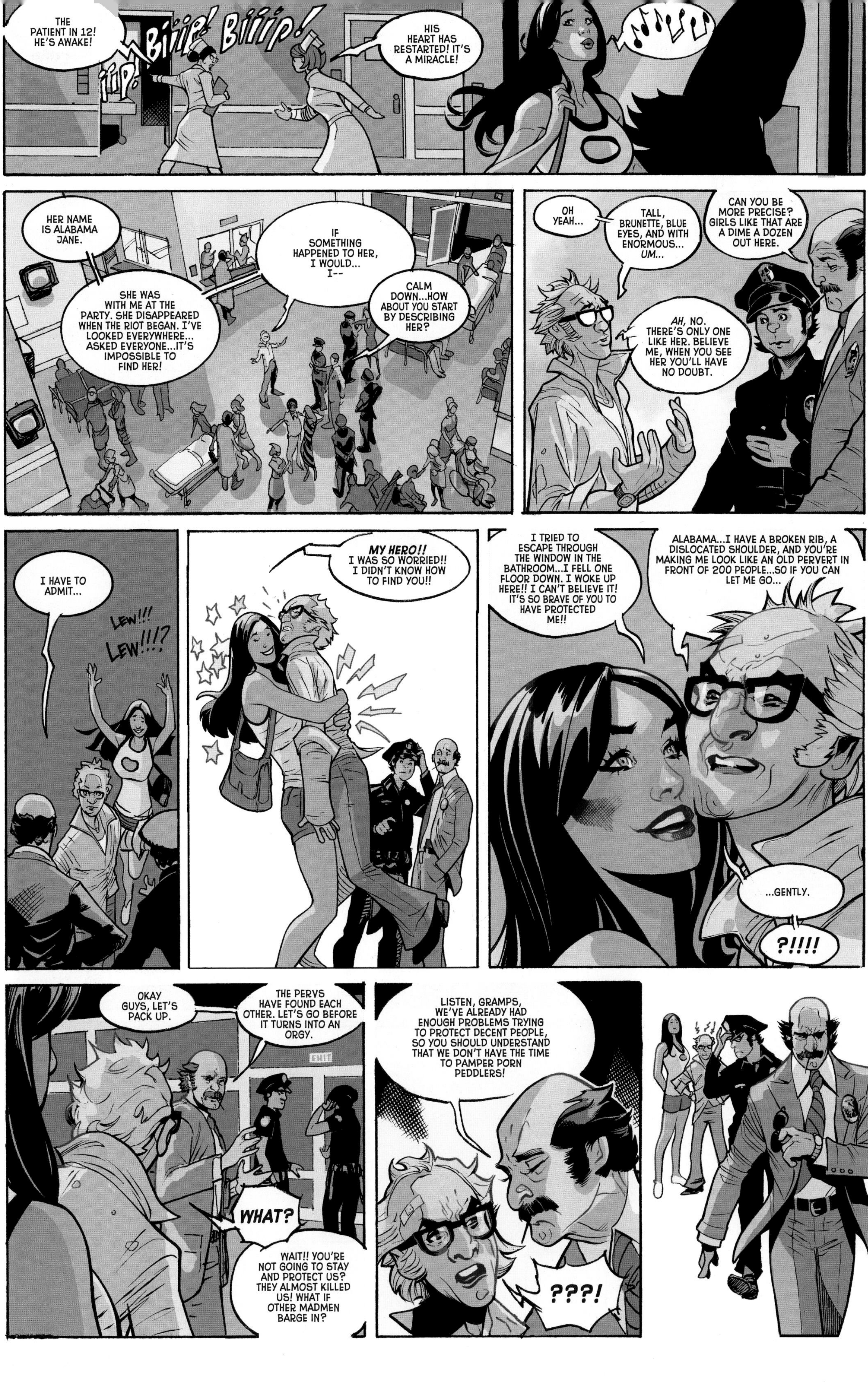
THE PATIENT IN 12! HE'S AWAKE!
iiip! Biiip! Biiip!
HIS HEART HAS RESTARTED! IT'S A MIRACLE!
HER NAME IS ALABAMA JANE.
SHE WAS WITH ME AT THE PARTY. SHE DISAPPEARED WHEN THE RIOT BEGAN. I'VE LOOKED EVERYWHERE... ASKED EVERYONE...IT'S IMPOSSIBLE TO FIND HER!
IF SOMETHING HAPPENED TO HER, I WOULD... I--
CALM DOWN...HOW ABOUT YOU START BY DESCRIBING HER?
OH YEAH...
TALL, BRUNETTE, BLUE EYES, AND WITH ENORMOUS... UM...
CAN YOU BE MORE PRECISE? GIRLS LIKE THAT ARE A DIME A DOZEN OUT HERE.
AH, NO. THERE'S ONLY ONE LIKE HER. BELIEVE ME, WHEN YOU SEE HER YOU'LL HAVE NO DOUBT.
I HAVE TO ADMIT...
LEW!!!
LEW!!!?
MY HERO!! I WAS SO WORRIED!! I DIDN'T KNOW HOW TO FIND YOU!!
I TRIED TO ESCAPE THROUGH THE WINDOW IN THE BATHROOM...I FELL ONE FLOOR DOWN. I WOKE UP HERE!! I CAN'T BELIEVE IT! IT'S SO BRAVE OF YOU TO HAVE PROTECTED ME!!
ALABAMA...I HAVE A BROKEN RIB, A DISLOCATED SHOULDER, AND YOU'RE MAKING ME LOOK LIKE AN OLD PERVERT IN FRONT OF 200 PEOPLE...SO IF YOU CAN LET ME GO...
...GENTLY.
?!!!!
OKAY GUYS, LET'S PACK UP.
THE PERVS HAVE FOUND EACH OTHER. LET'S GO BEFORE IT TURNS INTO AN ORGY.
EXIT
WHAT?
WAIT!! YOU'RE NOT GOING TO STAY AND PROTECT US? THEY ALMOST KILLED US! WHAT IF OTHER MADMEN BARGE IN?
LISTEN, GRAMPS, WE'VE ALREADY HAD ENOUGH PROBLEMS TRYING TO PROTECT DECENT PEOPLE, SO YOU SHOULD UNDERSTAND THAT WE DON'T HAVE THE TIME TO PAMPER PORN PEDDLERS!
???!

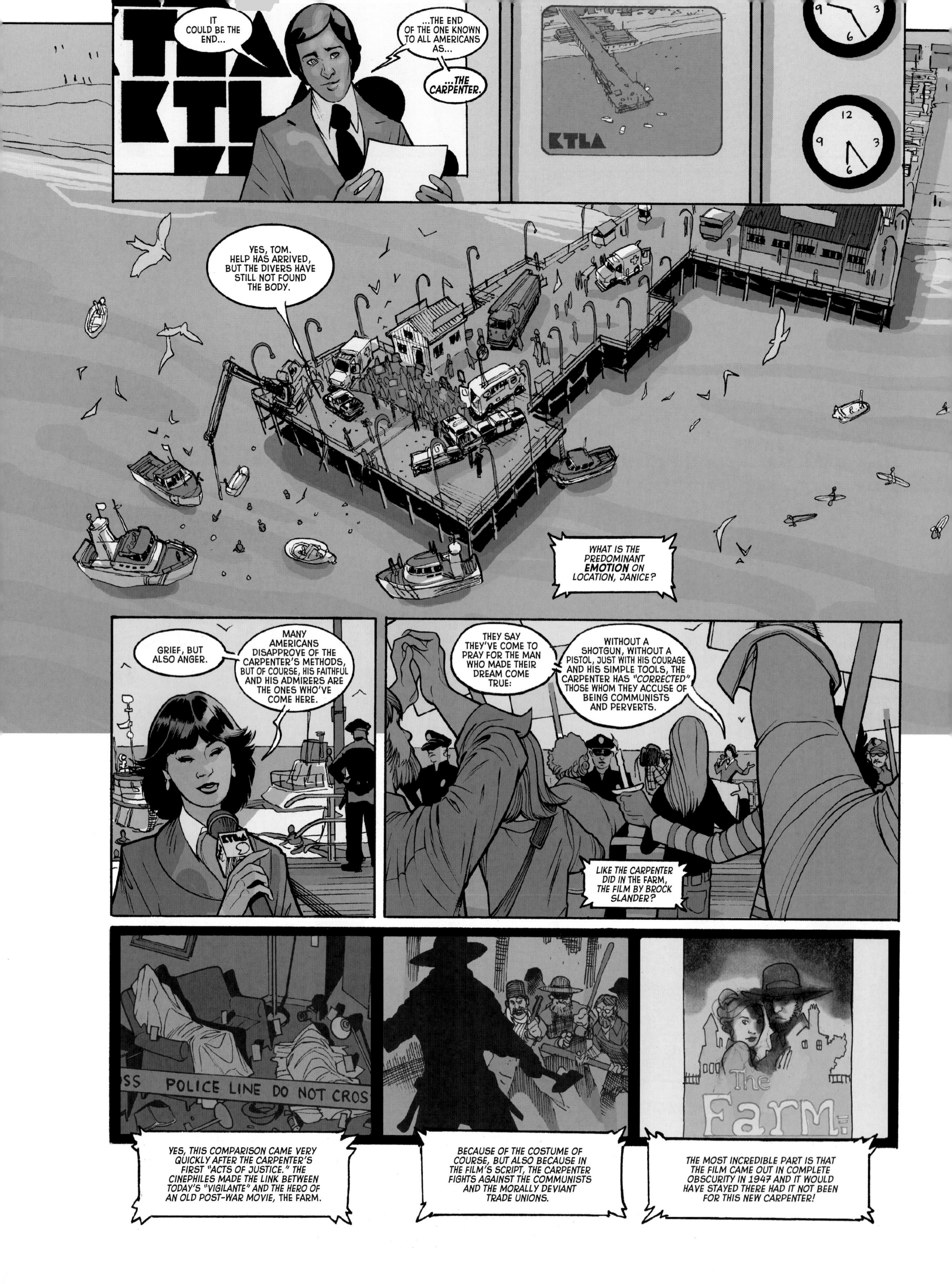

KTLA
IT COULD BE THE END...
...THE END OF THE ONE KNOWN TO ALL AMERICANS AS...
...THE CARPENTER.
KTLA
YES, TOM. HELP HAS ARRIVED, BUT THE DIVERS HAVE STILL NOT FOUND THE BODY.
WHAT IS THE PREDOMINANT EMOTION ON LOCATION, JANICE?
GRIEF, BUT ALSO ANGER.
MANY AMERICANS DISAPPROVE OF THE CARPENTER'S METHODS, BUT OF COURSE, HIS FAITHFUL AND HIS ADMIRERS ARE THE ONES WHO'VE COME HERE.
THEY SAY THEY'VE COME TO PRAY FOR THE MAN WHO MADE THEIR DREAM COME TRUE:
WITHOUT A SHOTGUN, WITHOUT A PISTOL, JUST WITH HIS COURAGE AND HIS SIMPLE TOOLS, THE CARPENTER HAS "CORRECTED" THOSE WHOM THEY ACCUSE OF BEING COMMUNISTS AND PERVERTS.
LIKE THE CARPENTER DID IN THE FARM, THE FILM BY BROCK SLANDER?
SS POLICE LINE DO NOT CROS
The Farm
YES, THIS COMPARISON CAME VERY QUICKLY AFTER THE CARPENTER'S FIRST "ACTS OF JUSTICE." THE CINEPHILES MADE THE LINK BETWEEN TODAY'S "VIGILANTE" AND THE HERO OF AN OLD POST-WAR MOVIE, THE FARM.
BECAUSE OF THE COSTUME OF COURSE, BUT ALSO BECAUSE IN THE FILM'S SCRIPT, THE CARPENTER FIGHTS AGAINST THE COMMUNISTS AND THE MORALLY DEVIANT TRADE UNIONS.
THE MOST INCREDIBLE PART IS THAT THE FILM CAME OUT IN COMPLETE OBSCURITY IN 1947 AND IT WOULD HAVE STAYED THERE HAD IT NOT BEEN FOR THIS NEW CARPENTER!

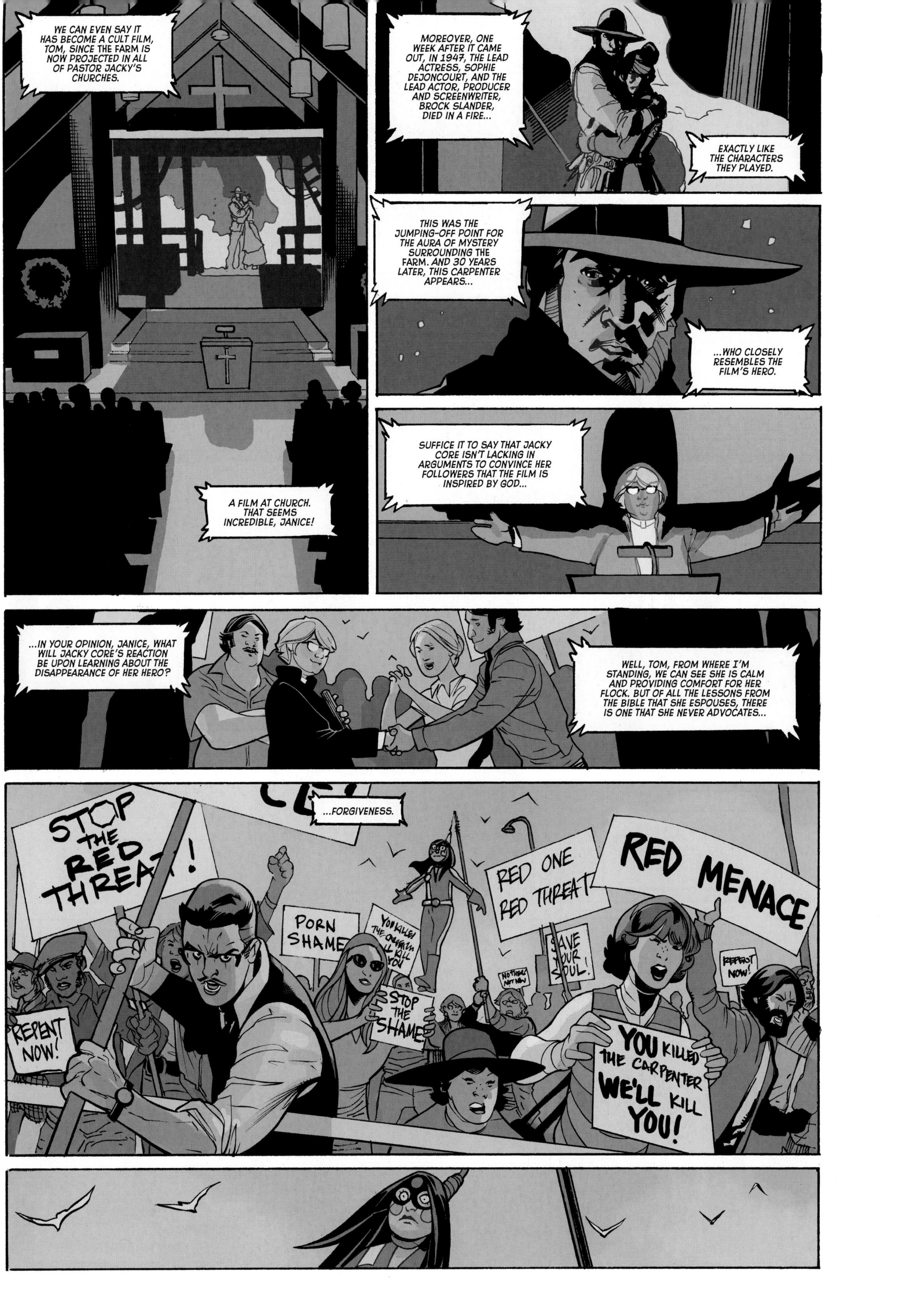
WE CAN EVEN SAY IT HAS BECOME A CULT FILM, TOM, SINCE THE FARM IS NOW PROJECTED IN ALL OF PASTOR JACKY'S CHURCHES.
A FILM AT CHURCH. THAT SEEMS INCREDIBLE, JANICE!
MOREOVER, ONE WEEK AFTER IT CAME OUT, IN 1947, THE LEAD ACTRESS, SOPHIE DEJONCOURT, AND THE LEAD ACTOR, PRODUCER AND SCREENWRITER, BROCK SLANDER, DIED IN A FIRE...
EXACTLY LIKE THE CHARACTERS THEY PLAYED.
THIS WAS THE JUMPING-OFF POINT FOR THE AURA OF MYSTERY SURROUNDING THE FARM. AND 30 YEARS LATER, THIS CARPENTER APPEARS...
...WHO CLOSELY RESEMBLES THE FILM'S HERO.
SUFFICE IT TO SAY THAT JACKY CORE ISN'T LACKING IN ARGUMENTS TO CONVINCE HER FOLLOWERS THAT THE FILM IS INSPIRED BY GOD...
...IN YOUR OPINION, JANICE, WHAT WILL JACKY CORE'S REACTION BE UPON LEARNING ABOUT THE DISAPPEARANCE OF HER HERO?
WELL, TOM, FROM WHERE I'M STANDING, WE CAN SEE SHE IS CALM AND PROVIDING COMFORT FOR HER FLOCK. BUT OF ALL THE LESSONS FROM THE BIBLE THAT SHE ESPOUSES, THERE IS ONE THAT SHE NEVER ADVOCATES...
...FORGIVENESS.
STOP THE RED THREAT!
RED ONE RED THREAT
RED MENACE
PORN SHAME
SAVE YOUR SOUL!
REPENT NOW!
STOP THE SHAME
REPENT NOW!
YOU KILLED THE CARPENTER WE'LL KILL YOU!

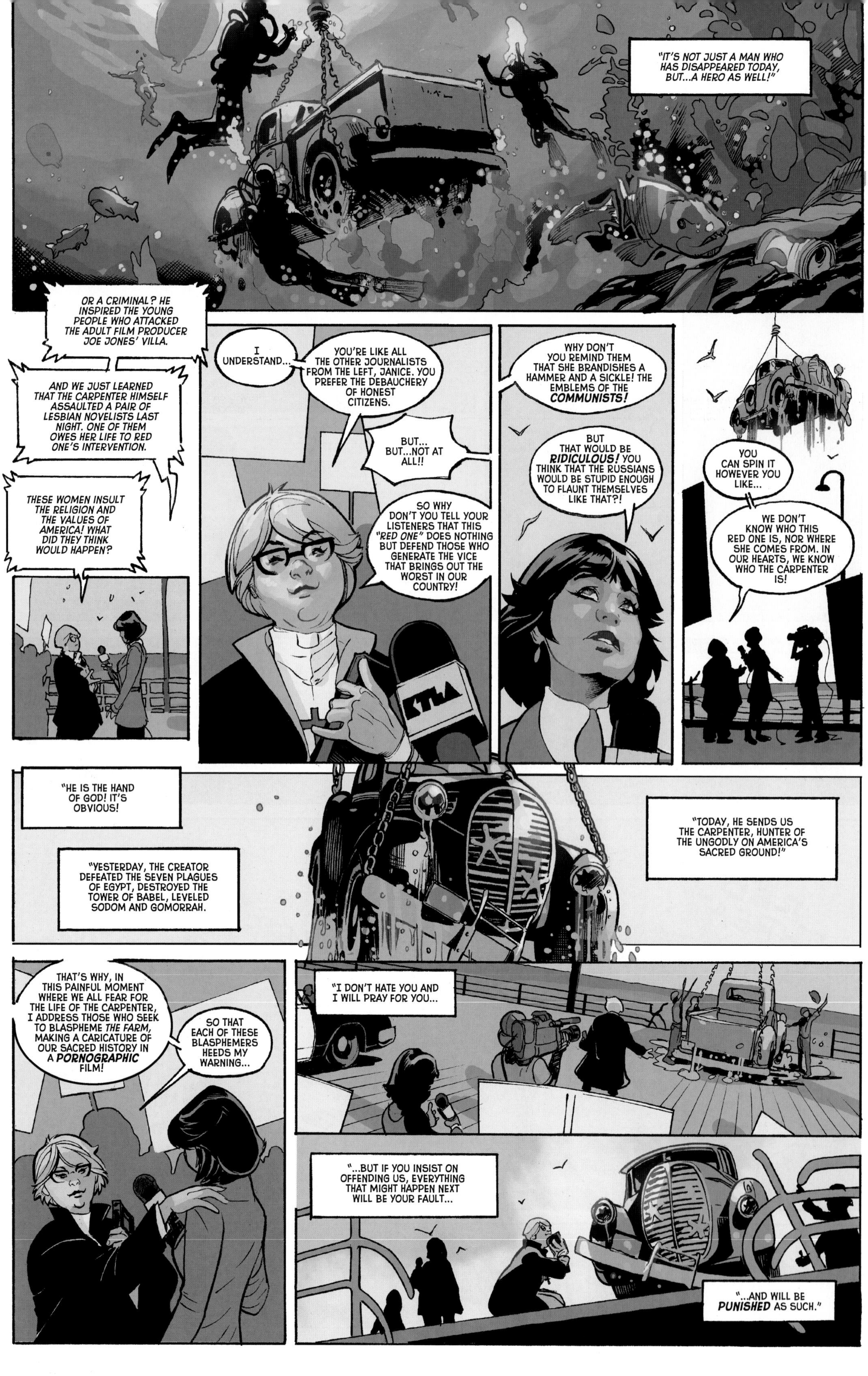

"IT'S NOT JUST A MAN WHO HAS DISAPPEARED TODAY, BUT...A HERO AS WELL!"
OR A CRIMINAL? HE INSPIRED THE YOUNG PEOPLE WHO ATTACKED THE ADULT FILM PRODUCER JOE JONES' VILLA.
AND WE JUST LEARNED THAT THE CARPENTER HIMSELF ASSAULTED A PAIR OF LESBIAN NOVELISTS LAST NIGHT. ONE OF THEM OWES HER LIFE TO RED ONE'S INTERVENTION.
THESE WOMEN INSULT THE RELIGION AND THE VALUES OF AMERICA! WHAT DID THEY THINK WOULD HAPPEN?
I UNDERSTAND...
YOU'RE LIKE ALL THE OTHER JOURNALISTS FROM THE LEFT, JANICE. YOU PREFER THE DEBAUCHERY OF HONEST CITIZENS.
BUT... BUT...NOT AT ALL!!
SO WHY DON'T YOU TELL YOUR LISTENERS THAT THIS "RED ONE" DOES NOTHING BUT DEFEND THOSE WHO GENERATE THE VICE THAT BRINGS OUT THE WORST IN OUR COUNTRY!
WHY DON'T YOU REMIND THEM THAT SHE BRANDISHES A HAMMER AND A SICKLE! THE EMBLEMS OF THE COMMUNISTS!
BUT THAT WOULD BE RIDICULOUS! YOU THINK THAT THE RUSSIANS WOULD BE STUPID ENOUGH TO FLAUNT THEMSELVES LIKE THAT?!
YOU CAN SPIN IT HOWEVER YOU LIKE...
WE DON'T KNOW WHO THIS RED ONE IS, NOR WHERE SHE COMES FROM. IN OUR HEARTS, WE KNOW WHO THE CARPENTER IS!
KTLA
"HE IS THE HAND OF GOD! IT'S OBVIOUS!
"YESTERDAY, THE CREATOR DEFEATED THE SEVEN PLAGUES OF EGYPT, DESTROYED THE TOWER OF BABEL, LEVELED SODOM AND GOMORRAH.
"TODAY, HE SENDS US THE CARPENTER, HUNTER OF THE UNGODLY ON AMERICA'S SACRED GROUND!"
THAT'S WHY, IN THIS PAINFUL MOMENT WHERE WE ALL FEAR FOR THE LIFE OF THE CARPENTER, I ADDRESS THOSE WHO SEEK TO BLASPHEME THE FARM, MAKING A CARICATURE OF OUR SACRED HISTORY IN A PORNOGRAPHIC FILM!
SO THAT EACH OF THESE BLASPHEMERS HEEDS MY WARNING...
"I DON'T HATE YOU AND I WILL PRAY FOR YOU...
"...BUT IF YOU INSIST ON OFFENDING US, EVERYTHING THAT MIGHT HAPPEN NEXT WILL BE YOUR FAULT...
"...AND WILL BE PUNISHED AS SUCH."

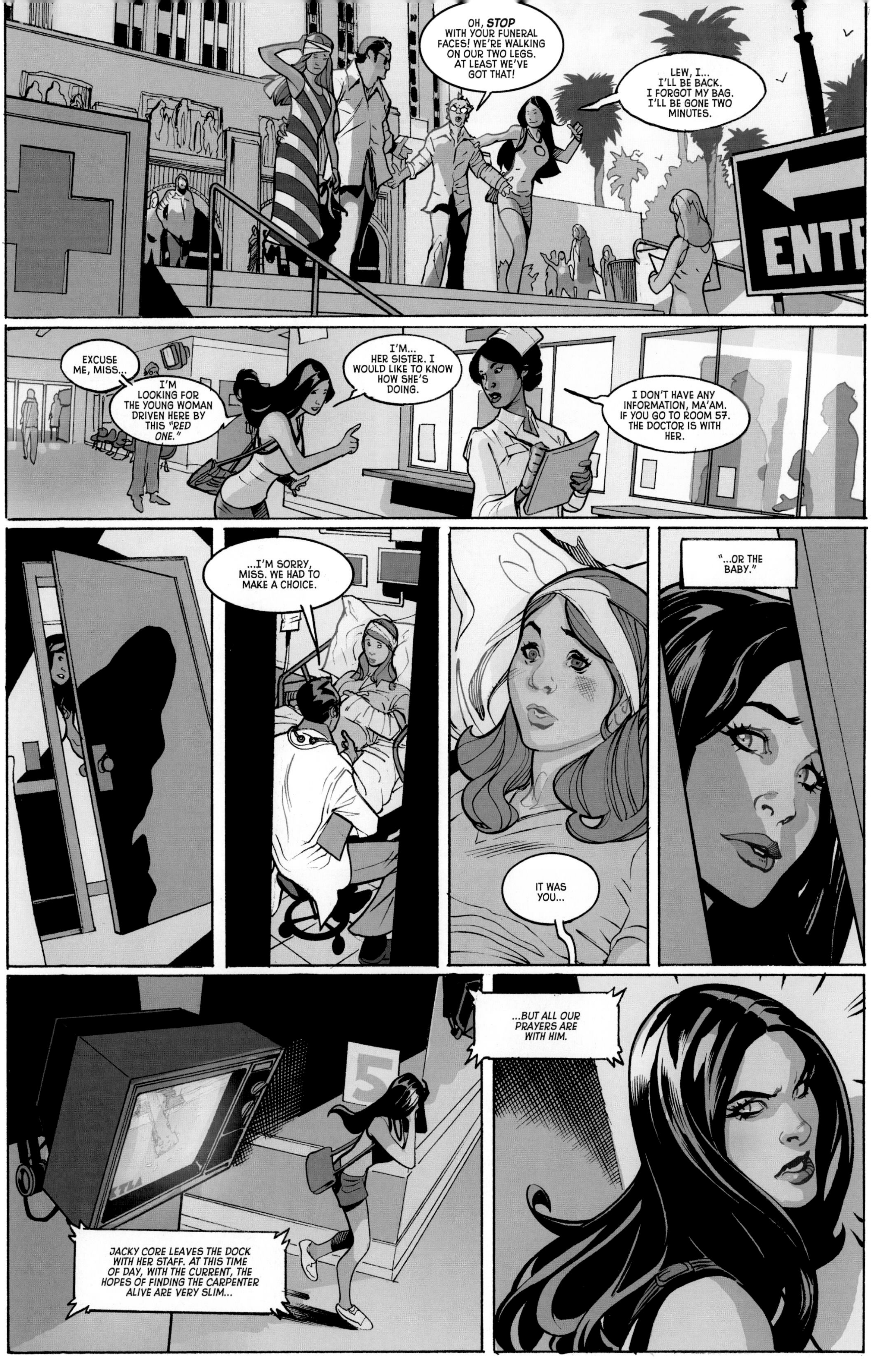
OH, STOP WITH YOUR FUNERAL FACES! WE'RE WALKING ON OUR TWO LEGS. AT LEAST WE'VE GOT THAT!
LEW, I... I'LL BE BACK. I FORGOT MY BAG. I'LL BE GONE TWO MINUTES.
ENTE
EXCUSE ME, MISS...
I'M LOOKING FOR THE YOUNG WOMAN DRIVEN HERE BY THIS "RED ONE."
I'M... HER SISTER. I WOULD LIKE TO KNOW HOW SHE'S DOING.
I DON'T HAVE ANY INFORMATION, MA'AM. IF YOU GO TO ROOM 57. THE DOCTOR IS WITH HER.
...I'M SORRY, MISS. WE HAD TO MAKE A CHOICE.
IT WAS YOU...
"...OR THE BABY."
JACKY CORE LEAVES THE DOCK WITH HER STAFF. AT THIS TIME OF DAY, WITH THE CURRENT, THE HOPES OF FINDING THE CARPENTER ALIVE ARE VERY SLIM...
...BUT ALL OUR PRAYERS ARE WITH HIM.

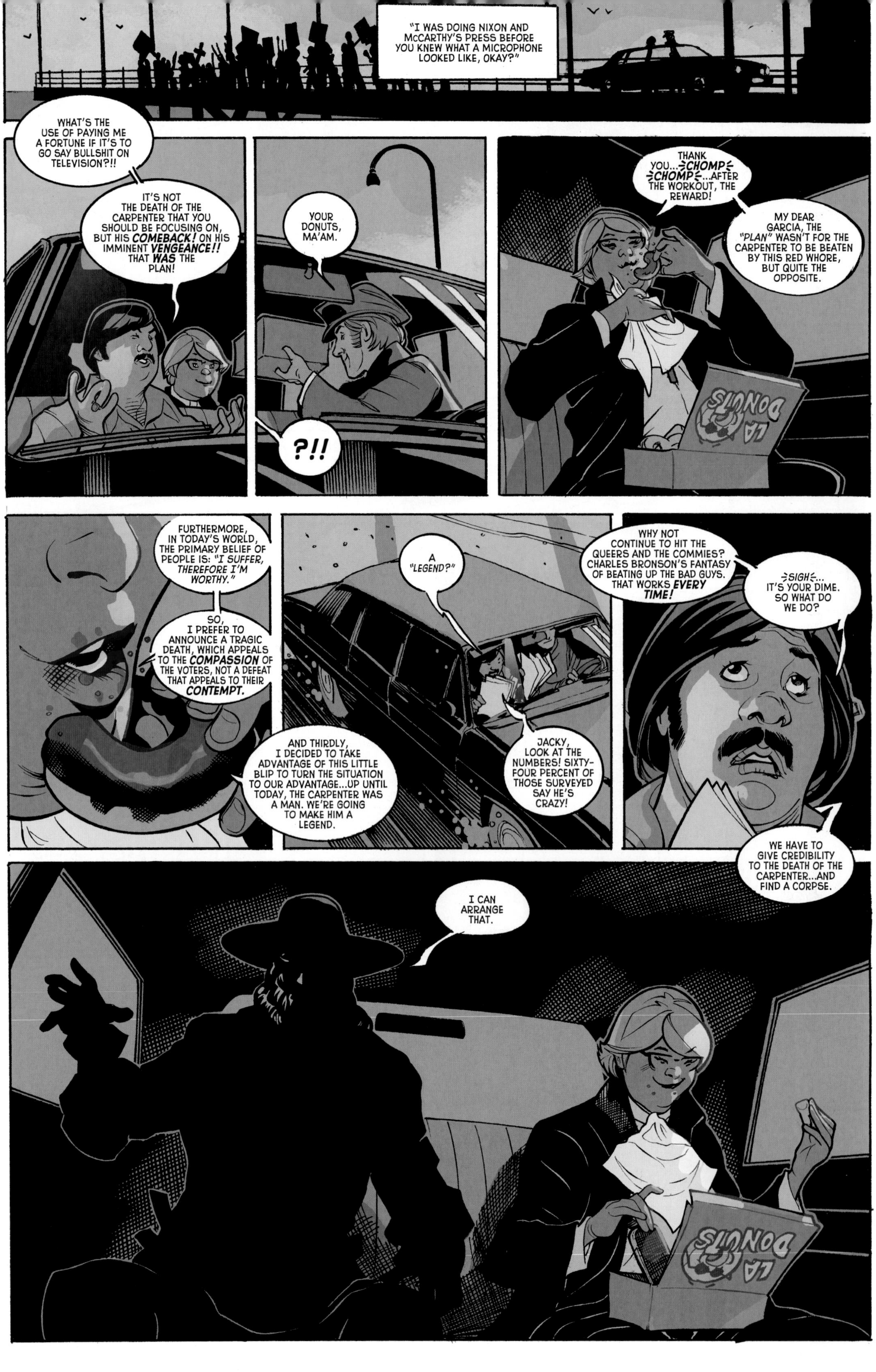
"I WAS DOING NIXON AND McCARTHY'S PRESS BEFORE YOU KNEW WHAT A MICROPHONE LOOKED LIKE, OKAY?"
WHAT'S THE USE OF PAYING ME A FORTUNE IF IT'S TO GO SAY BULLSHIT ON TELEVISION?!!
IT'S NOT THE DEATH OF THE CARPENTER THAT YOU SHOULD BE FOCUSING ON, BUT HIS COMEBACK! ON HIS IMMINENT VENGEANCE!! THAT WAS THE PLAN!
YOUR DONUTS, MA'AM.
?!!
THANK YOU... CHOMP CHOMP ...AFTER THE WORKOUT, THE REWARD!
MY DEAR GARCIA, THE "PLAN" WASN'T FOR THE CARPENTER TO BE BEATEN BY THIS RED WHORE, BUT QUITE THE OPPOSITE.
LA DONUTS
FURTHERMORE, IN TODAY'S WORLD, THE PRIMARY BELIEF OF PEOPLE IS: "I SUFFER, THEREFORE I'M WORTHY."
SO, I PREFER TO ANNOUNCE A TRAGIC DEATH, WHICH APPEALS TO THE COMPASSION OF THE VOTERS, NOT A DEFEAT THAT APPEALS TO THEIR CONTEMPT.
AND THIRDLY, I DECIDED TO TAKE ADVANTAGE OF THIS LITTLE BLIP TO TURN THE SITUATION TO OUR ADVANTAGE...UP UNTIL TODAY, THE CARPENTER WAS A MAN. WE'RE GOING TO MAKE HIM A LEGEND.
A "LEGEND?"
JACKY, LOOK AT THE NUMBERS! SIXTY-FOUR PERCENT OF THOSE SURVEYED SAY HE'S CRAZY!
WHY NOT CONTINUE TO HIT THE QUEERS AND THE COMMIES? CHARLES BRONSON'S FANTASY OF BEATING UP THE BAD GUYS. THAT WORKS EVERY TIME!
SIGH... IT'S YOUR DIME. SO WHAT DO WE DO?
WE HAVE TO GIVE CREDIBILITY TO THE DEATH OF THE CARPENTER...AND FIND A CORPSE.
I CAN ARRANGE THAT.
LA DONUTS

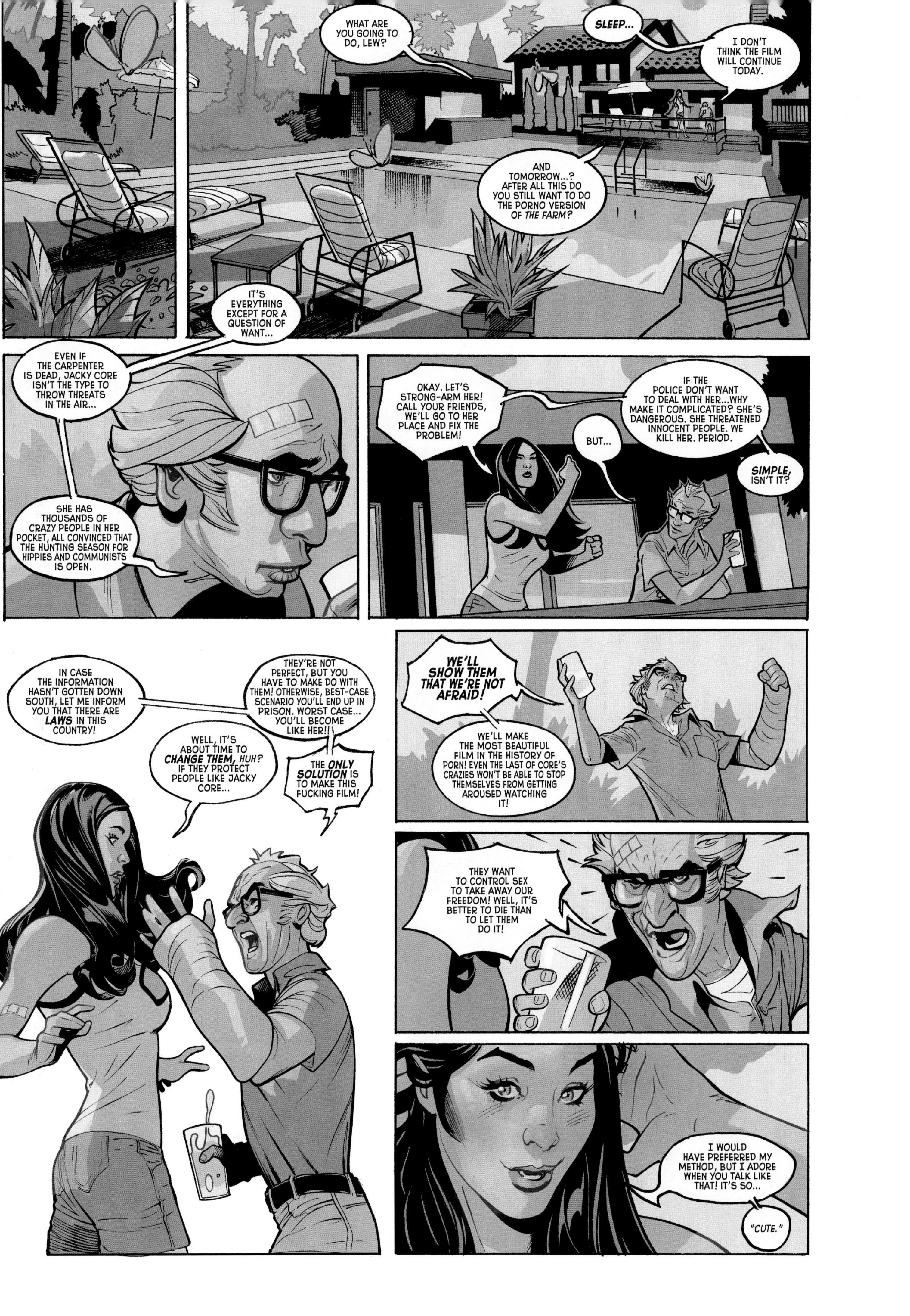
WHAT ARE YOU GOING TO DO, LEW?
SLEEP...
I DON'T THINK THE FILM WILL CONTINUE TODAY.
AND TOMORROW...? AFTER ALL THIS DO YOU STILL WANT TO DO THE PORNO VERSION OF THE FARM?
IT'S EVERYTHING EXCEPT FOR A QUESTION OF WANT...
EVEN IF THE CARPENTER IS DEAD, JACKY CORE ISN'T THE TYPE TO THROW THREATS IN THE AIR...
SHE HAS THOUSANDS OF CRAZY PEOPLE IN HER POCKET, ALL CONVINCED THAT THE HUNTING SEASON FOR HIPPIES AND COMMUNISTS IS OPEN.
OKAY. LET'S STRONG-ARM HER! CALL YOUR FRIENDS, WE'LL GO TO HER PLACE AND FIX THE PROBLEM!
BUT...
IF THE POLICE DON'T WANT TO DEAL WITH HER...WHY MAKE IT COMPLICATED? SHE'S DANGEROUS. SHE THREATENED INNOCENT PEOPLE. WE KILL HER. PERIOD.
SIMPLE, ISN'T IT?
IN CASE THE INFORMATION HASN'T GOTTEN DOWN SOUTH, LET ME INFORM YOU THAT THERE ARE LAWS IN THIS COUNTRY!
THEY'RE NOT PERFECT, BUT YOU HAVE TO MAKE DO WITH THEM! OTHERWISE, BEST-CASE SCENARIO YOU'LL END UP IN PRISON. WORST CASE... YOU'LL BECOME LIKE HER!!
WELL, IT'S ABOUT TIME TO CHANGE THEM, HUH? IF THEY PROTECT PEOPLE LIKE JACKY CORE...
THE ONLY SOLUTION IS TO MAKE THIS FUCKING FILM!
WE'LL SHOW THEM THAT WE'RE NOT AFRAID!
WE'LL MAKE THE MOST BEAUTIFUL FILM IN THE HISTORY OF PORN! EVEN THE LAST OF CORE'S CRAZIES WON'T BE ABLE TO STOP THEMSELVES FROM GETTING AROUSED WATCHING IT!
THEY WANT TO CONTROL SEX TO TAKE AWAY OUR FREEDOM! WELL, IT'S BETTER TO DIE THAN TO LET THEM DO IT!
I WOULD HAVE PREFERRED MY METHOD, BUT I ADORE WHEN YOU TALK LIKE THAT! IT'S SO...
"CUTE."

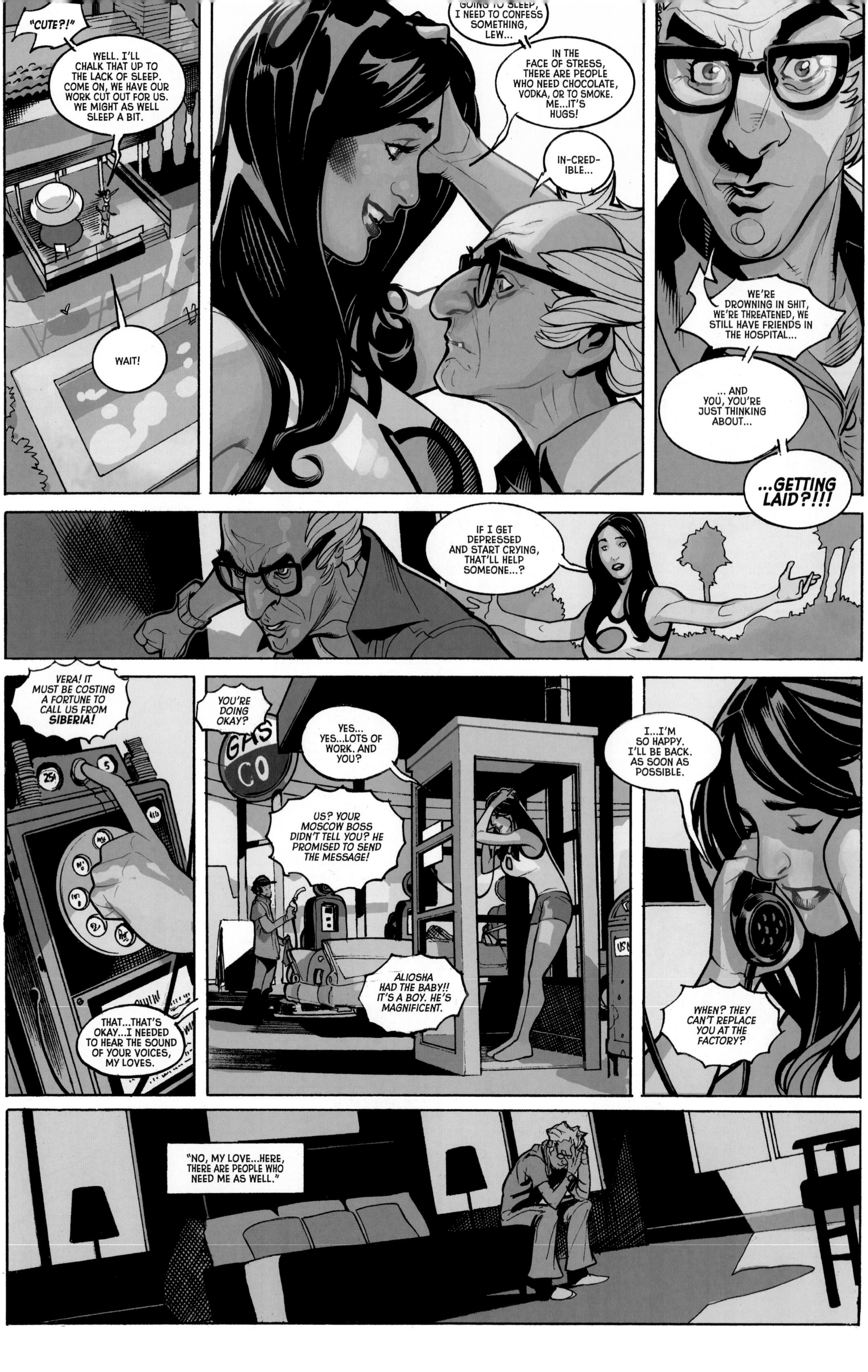

"CUTE?!"
WELL. I'LL CHALK THAT UP TO THE LACK OF SLEEP. COME ON, WE HAVE OUR WORK CUT OUT FOR US. WE MIGHT AS WELL SLEEP A BIT.
WAIT!
GOING TO SLEEP, I NEED TO CONFESS SOMETHING, LEW...
IN THE FACE OF STRESS, THERE ARE PEOPLE WHO NEED CHOCOLATE, VODKA, OR TO SMOKE. ME...IT'S HUGS!
IN-CRED-IBLE...
WE'RE DROWNING IN SHIT, WE'RE THREATENED, WE STILL HAVE FRIENDS IN THE HOSPITAL...
... AND YOU, YOU'RE JUST THINKING ABOUT...
...GETTING LAID?!!!
IF I GET DEPRESSED AND START CRYING, THAT'LL HELP SOMEONE...?
VERA! IT MUST BE COSTING A FORTUNE TO CALL US FROM SIBERIA!
THAT...THAT'S OKAY...I NEEDED TO HEAR THE SOUND OF YOUR VOICES, MY LOVES.
YOU'RE DOING OKAY?
YES... YES...LOTS OF WORK. AND YOU?
US? YOUR MOSCOW BOSS DIDN'T TELL YOU? HE PROMISED TO SEND THE MESSAGE!
ALIOSHA HAD THE BABY!! IT'S A BOY. HE'S MAGNIFICENT.
I...I'M SO HAPPY. I'LL BE BACK. AS SOON AS POSSIBLE.
WHEN? THEY CAN'T REPLACE YOU AT THE FACTORY?
"NO, MY LOVE...HERE, THERE ARE PEOPLE WHO NEED ME AS WELL."

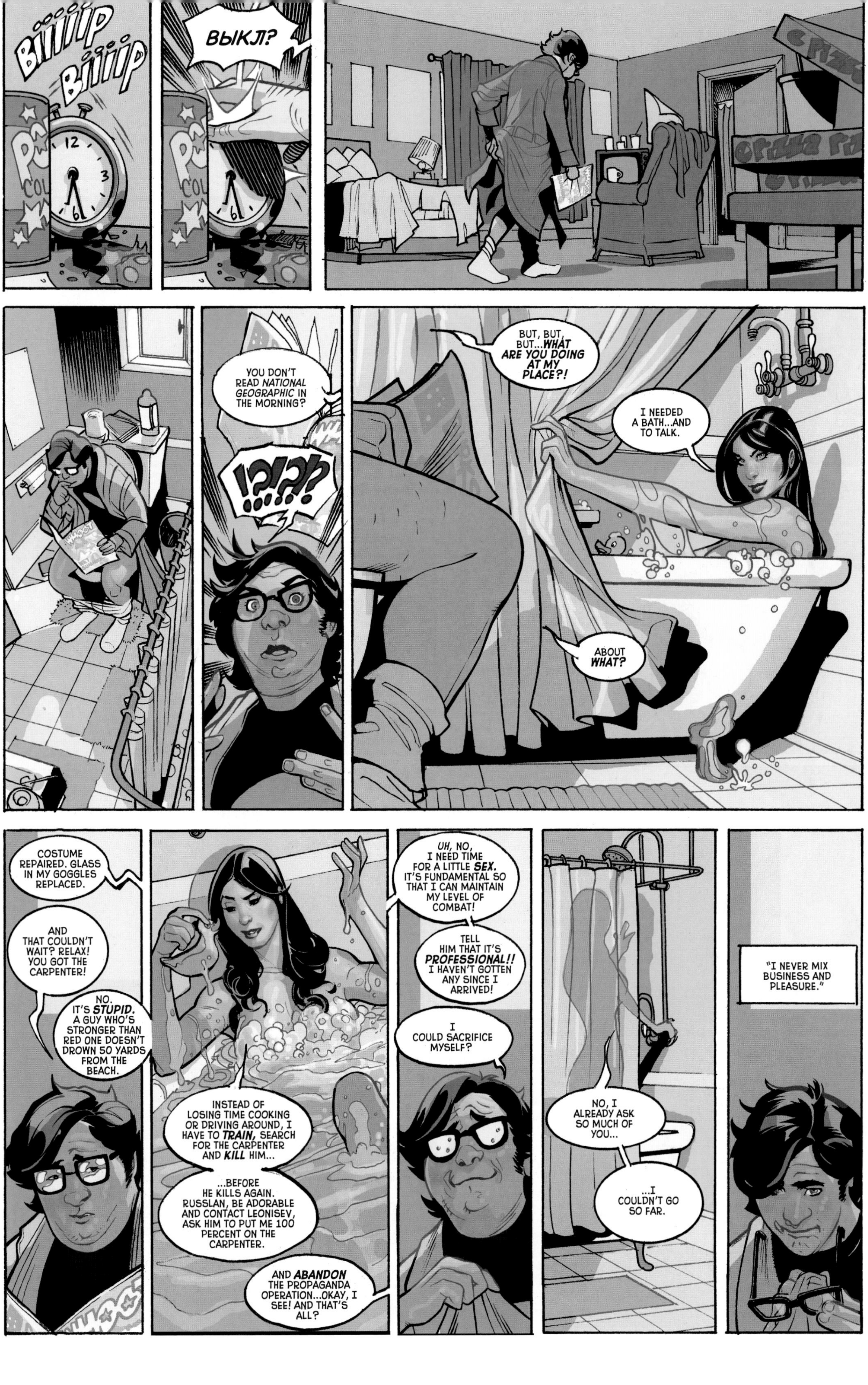
BIIIIP
BIIIIP
ВЫКЛ?
YOU DON'T READ NATIONAL GEOGRAPHIC IN THE MORNING?
!?!?!?
BUT, BUT, BUT...WHAT ARE YOU DOING AT MY PLACE?!
I NEEDED A BATH...AND TO TALK.
ABOUT WHAT?
COSTUME REPAIRED. GLASS IN MY GOGGLES REPLACED.
AND THAT COULDN'T WAIT? RELAX! YOU GOT THE CARPENTER!
NO. IT'S STUPID. A GUY WHO'S STRONGER THAN RED ONE DOESN'T DROWN 50 YARDS FROM THE BEACH.
INSTEAD OF LOSING TIME COOKING OR DRIVING AROUND, I HAVE TO TRAIN, SEARCH FOR THE CARPENTER AND KILL HIM...
...BEFORE HE KILLS AGAIN. RUSSLAN, BE ADORABLE AND CONTACT LEONISEV, ASK HIM TO PUT ME 100 PERCENT ON THE CARPENTER.
AND ABANDON THE PROPAGANDA OPERATION...OKAY, I SEE! AND THAT'S ALL?
UH, NO, I NEED TIME FOR A LITTLE SEX. IT'S FUNDAMENTAL SO THAT I CAN MAINTAIN MY LEVEL OF COMBAT!
TELL HIM THAT IT'S PROFESSIONAL!! I HAVEN'T GOTTEN ANY SINCE I ARRIVED!
I COULD SACRIFICE MYSELF?
NO, I ALREADY ASK SO MUCH OF YOU...
...I COULDN'T GO SO FAR.
"I NEVER MIX BUSINESS AND PLEASURE."

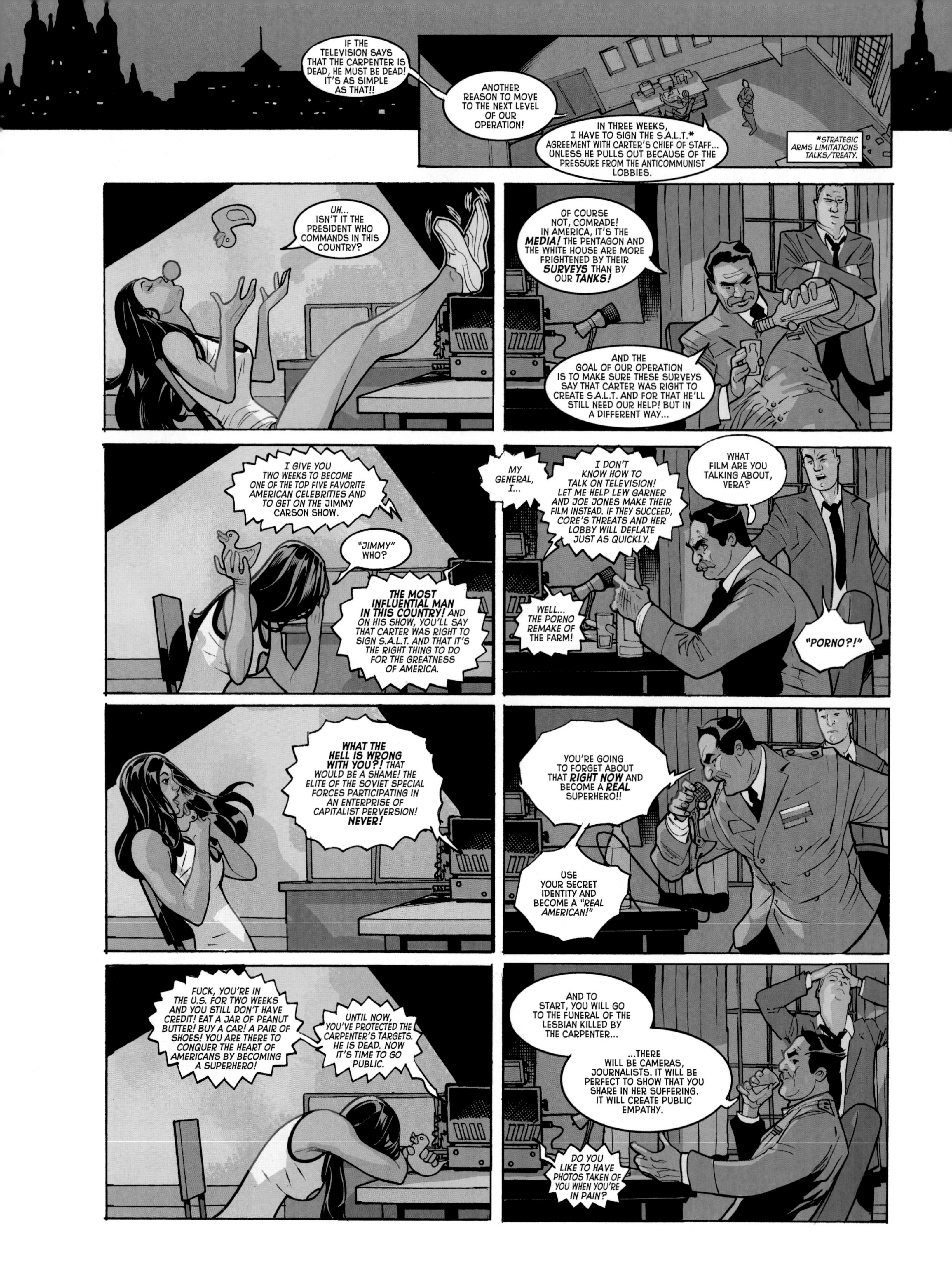
IF THE TELEVISION SAYS THAT THE CARPENTER IS DEAD, HE MUST BE DEAD! IT'S AS SIMPLE AS THAT!!
ANOTHER REASON TO MOVE TO THE NEXT LEVEL OF OUR OPERATION!
IN THREE WEEKS, I HAVE TO SIGN THE S.A.L.T.* AGREEMENT WITH CARTER'S CHIEF OF STAFF... UNLESS HE PULLS OUT BECAUSE OF THE PRESSURE FROM THE ANTICOMMUNIST LOBBIES.
*STRATEGIC ARMS LIMITATIONS TALKS/TREATY.
UH... ISN'T IT THE PRESIDENT WHO COMMANDS IN THIS COUNTRY?
OF COURSE NOT, COMRADE! IN AMERICA, IT'S THE MEDIA! THE PENTAGON AND THE WHITE HOUSE ARE MORE FRIGHTENED BY THEIR SURVEYS THAN BY OUR TANKS!
AND THE GOAL OF OUR OPERATION IS TO MAKE SURE THESE SURVEYS SAY THAT CARTER WAS RIGHT TO CREATE S.A.L.T. AND FOR THAT HE'LL STILL NEED OUR HELP! BUT IN A DIFFERENT WAY...
I GIVE YOU TWO WEEKS TO BECOME ONE OF THE TOP FIVE FAVORITE AMERICAN CELEBRITIES AND TO GET ON THE JIMMY CARSON SHOW.
"JIMMY" WHO?
THE MOST INFLUENTIAL MAN IN THIS COUNTRY! AND ON HIS SHOW, YOU'LL SAY THAT CARTER WAS RIGHT TO SIGN S.A.L.T. AND THAT IT'S THE RIGHT THING TO DO FOR THE GREATNESS OF AMERICA.
MY GENERAL, I...
I DON'T KNOW HOW TO TALK ON TELEVISION! LET ME HELP LEW GARNER AND JOE JONES MAKE THEIR FILM INSTEAD. IF THEY SUCCEED, CORE'S THREATS AND HER LOBBY WILL DEFLATE JUST AS QUICKLY.
WHAT FILM ARE YOU TALKING ABOUT, VERA?
WELL... THE PORNO REMAKE OF THE FARM!
"PORNO?!"
WHAT THE HELL IS WRONG WITH YOU?! THAT WOULD BE A SHAME! THE ELITE OF THE SOVIET SPECIAL FORCES PARTICIPATING IN AN ENTERPRISE OF CAPITALIST PERVERSION! NEVER!
YOU'RE GOING TO FORGET ABOUT THAT RIGHT NOW AND BECOME A REAL SUPERHERO!!
USE YOUR SECRET IDENTITY AND BECOME A "REAL AMERICAN!"
FUCK, YOU'RE IN THE U.S. FOR TWO WEEKS AND YOU STILL DON'T HAVE CREDIT! EAT A JAR OF PEANUT BUTTER! BUY A CAR! A PAIR OF SHOES! YOU ARE THERE TO CONQUER THE HEART OF AMERICANS BY BECOMING A SUPERHERO!
UNTIL NOW, YOU'VE PROTECTED THE CARPENTER'S TARGETS. HE IS DEAD. NOW IT'S TIME TO GO PUBLIC.
AND TO START, YOU WILL GO TO THE FUNERAL OF THE LESBIAN KILLED BY THE CARPENTER...
...THERE WILL BE CAMERAS, JOURNALISTS. IT WILL BE PERFECT TO SHOW THAT YOU SHARE IN HER SUFFERING. IT WILL CREATE PUBLIC EMPATHY.
DO YOU LIKE TO HAVE PHOTOS TAKEN OF YOU WHEN YOU'RE IN PAIN?

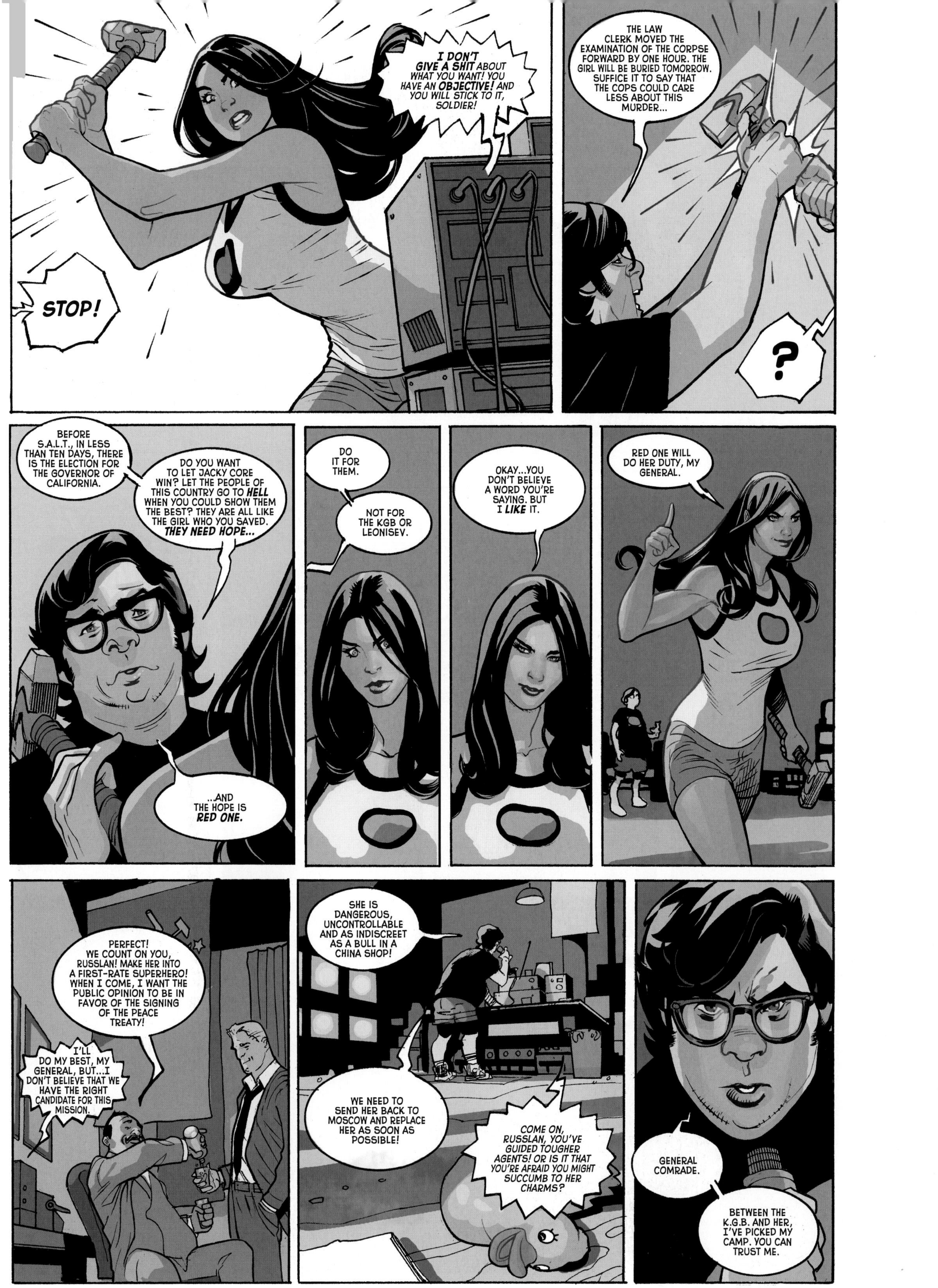
I DON'T GIVE A SHIT ABOUT WHAT YOU WANT! YOU HAVE AN OBJECTIVE! AND YOU WILL STICK TO IT, SOLDIER!
STOP!
THE LAW CLERK MOVED THE EXAMINATION OF THE CORPSE FORWARD BY ONE HOUR. THE GIRL WILL BE BURIED TOMORROW. SUFFICE IT TO SAY THAT THE COPS COULD CARE LESS ABOUT THIS MURDER...
?
BEFORE S.A.L.T., IN LESS THAN TEN DAYS, THERE IS THE ELECTION FOR THE GOVERNOR OF CALIFORNIA.
DO YOU WANT TO LET JACKY CORE WIN? LET THE PEOPLE OF THIS COUNTRY GO TO HELL WHEN YOU COULD SHOW THEM THE BEST? THEY ARE ALL LIKE THE GIRL WHO YOU SAVED. THEY NEED HOPE...
...AND THE HOPE IS RED ONE.
DO IT FOR THEM.
NOT FOR THE KGB OR LEONISEV.
OKAY...YOU DON'T BELIEVE A WORD YOU'RE SAYING. BUT I LIKE IT.
RED ONE WILL DO HER DUTY, MY GENERAL.
PERFECT! WE COUNT ON YOU, RUSSLAN! MAKE HER INTO A FIRST-RATE SUPERHERO! WHEN I COME, I WANT THE PUBLIC OPINION TO BE IN FAVOR OF THE SIGNING OF THE PEACE TREATY!
I'LL DO MY BEST, MY GENERAL, BUT...I DON'T BELIEVE THAT WE HAVE THE RIGHT CANDIDATE FOR THIS MISSION.
SHE IS DANGEROUS, UNCONTROLLABLE AND AS INDISCREET AS A BULL IN A CHINA SHOP!
WE NEED TO SEND HER BACK TO MOSCOW AND REPLACE HER AS SOON AS POSSIBLE!
COME ON, RUSSLAN, YOU'VE GUIDED TOUGHER AGENTS! OR IS IT THAT YOU'RE AFRAID YOU MIGHT SUCCUMB TO HER CHARMS?
GENERAL COMRADE.
BETWEEN THE K.G.B. AND HER, I'VE PICKED MY CAMP. YOU CAN TRUST ME.

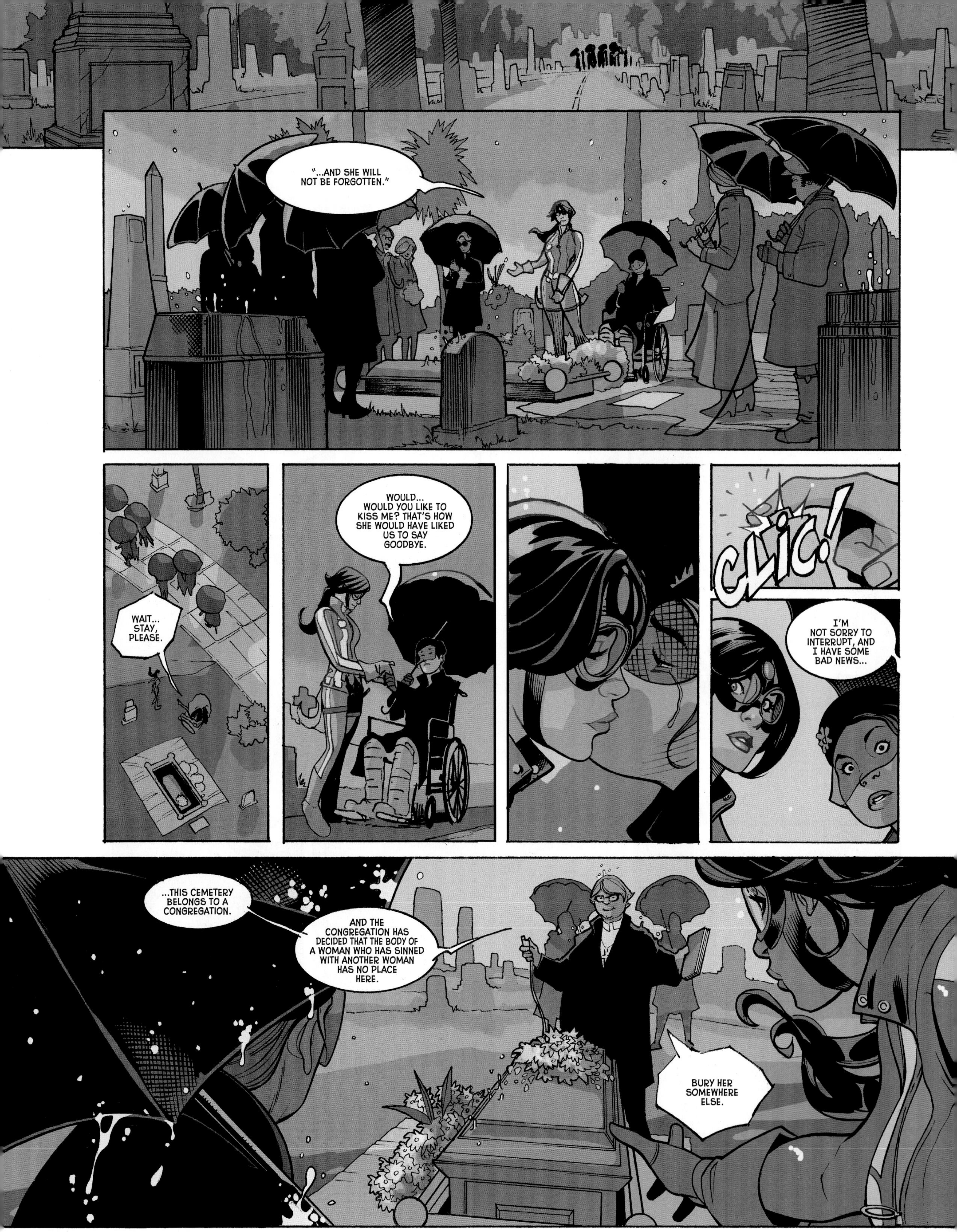
"...AND SHE WILL NOT BE FORGOTTEN."
WAIT... STAY, PLEASE.
WOULD... WOULD YOU LIKE TO KISS ME? THAT'S HOW SHE WOULD HAVE LIKED US TO SAY GOODBYE.
CLIC!
I'M NOT SORRY TO INTERRUPT, AND I HAVE SOME BAD NEWS...
...THIS CEMETERY BELONGS TO A CONGREGATION.
AND THE CONGREGATION HAS DECIDED THAT THE BODY OF A WOMAN WHO HAS SINNED WITH ANOTHER WOMAN HAS NO PLACE HERE.
BURY HER SOMEWHERE ELSE.

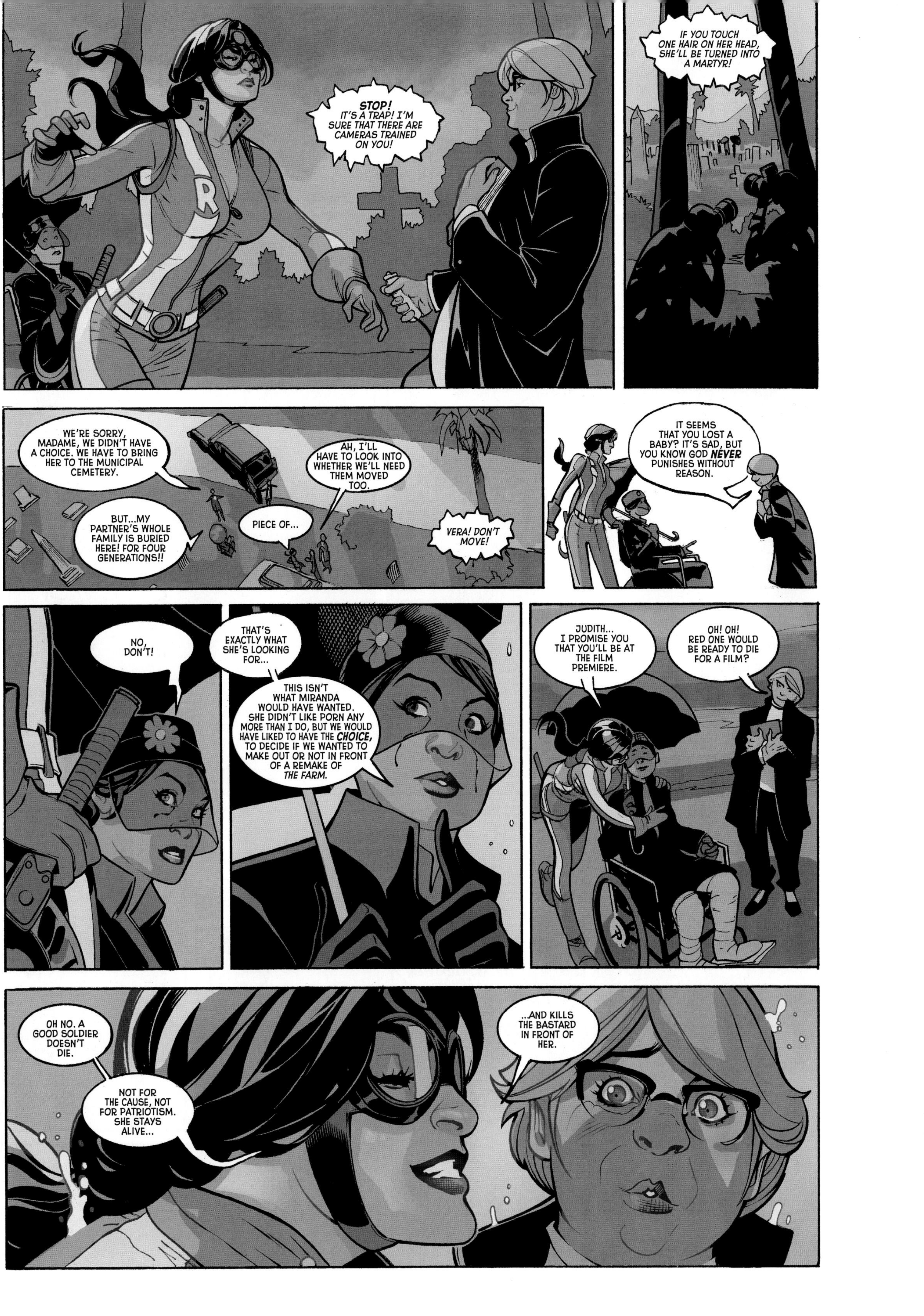
STOP! IT'S A TRAP! I'M SURE THAT THERE ARE CAMERAS TRAINED ON YOU!
IF YOU TOUCH ONE HAIR ON HER HEAD, SHE'LL BE TURNED INTO A MARTYR!
WE'RE SORRY, MADAME, WE DIDN'T HAVE A CHOICE. WE HAVE TO BRING HER TO THE MUNICIPAL CEMETERY.
AH, I'LL HAVE TO LOOK INTO WHETHER WE'LL NEED THEM MOVED TOO.
BUT...MY PARTNER'S WHOLE FAMILY IS BURIED HERE! FOR FOUR GENERATIONS!!
PIECE OF...
VERA! DON'T MOVE!
IT SEEMS THAT YOU LOST A BABY? IT'S SAD, BUT YOU KNOW GOD NEVER PUNISHES WITHOUT REASON.
NO, DON'T!
THAT'S EXACTLY WHAT SHE'S LOOKING FOR...
THIS ISN'T WHAT MIRANDA WOULD HAVE WANTED. SHE DIDN'T LIKE PORN ANY MORE THAN I DO, BUT WE WOULD HAVE LIKED TO HAVE THE CHOICE, TO DECIDE IF WE WANTED TO MAKE OUT OR NOT IN FRONT OF A REMAKE OF THE FARM.
JUDITH... I PROMISE YOU THAT YOU'LL BE AT THE FILM PREMIERE.
OH! OH! RED ONE WOULD BE READY TO DIE FOR A FILM?
OH NO. A GOOD SOLDIER DOESN'T DIE.
NOT FOR THE CAUSE, NOT FOR PATRIOTISM. SHE STAYS ALIVE...
...AND KILLS THE BASTARD IN FRONT OF HER.

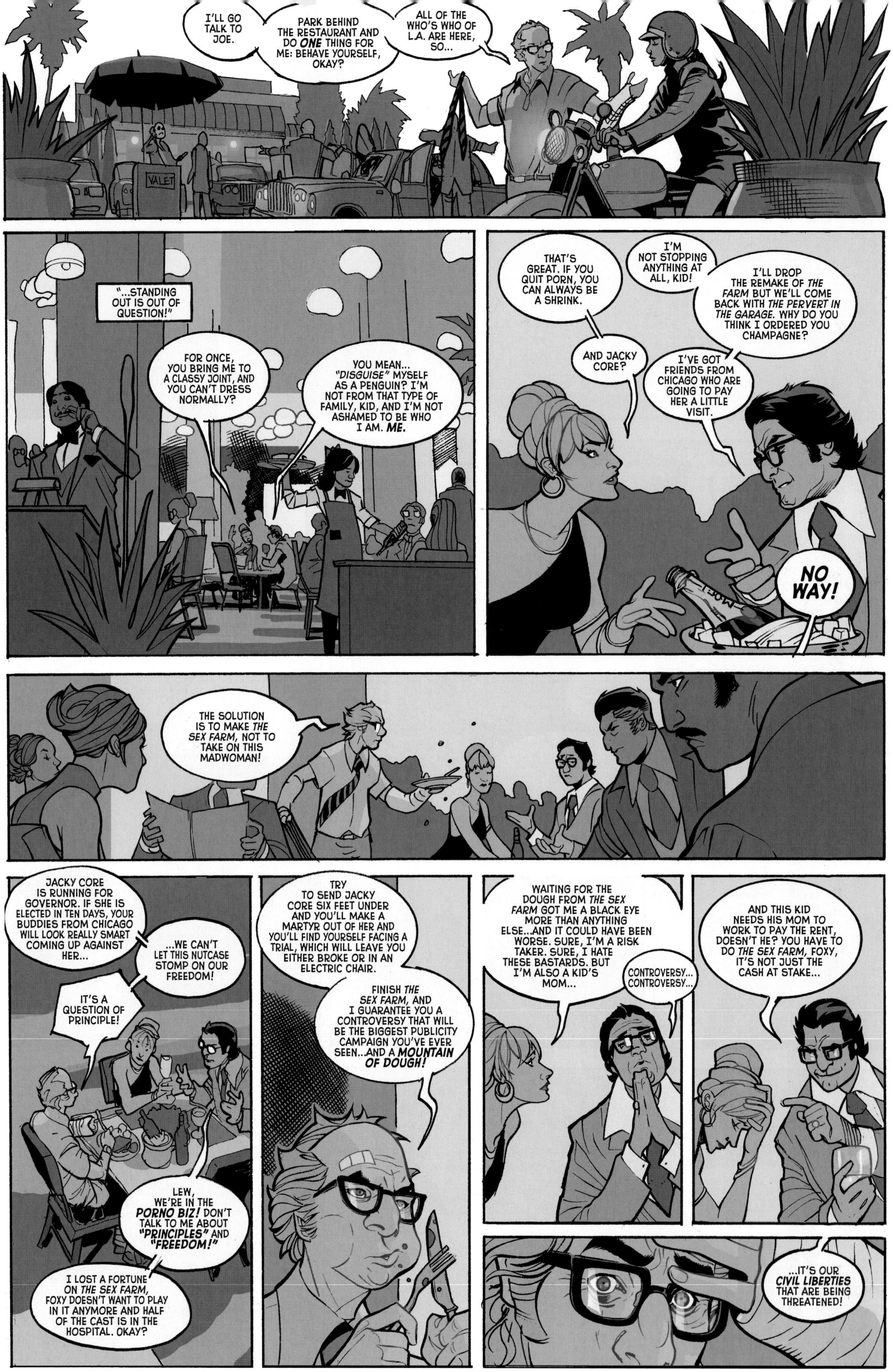
I'LL GO TALK TO JOE.
PARK BEHIND THE RESTAURANT AND DO ONE THING FOR ME: BEHAVE YOURSELF, OKAY?
ALL OF THE WHO'S WHO OF L.A. ARE HERE, SO...
VALET
"...STANDING OUT IS OUT OF QUESTION!"
FOR ONCE, YOU BRING ME TO A CLASSY JOINT, AND YOU CAN'T DRESS NORMALLY?
YOU MEAN... "DISGUISE" MYSELF AS A PENGUIN? I'M NOT FROM THAT TYPE OF FAMILY, KID, AND I'M NOT ASHAMED TO BE WHO I AM. ME.
THAT'S GREAT. IF YOU QUIT PORN, YOU CAN ALWAYS BE A SHRINK.
I'M NOT STOPPING ANYTHING AT ALL, KID!
I'LL DROP THE REMAKE OF THE FARM BUT WE'LL COME BACK WITH THE PERVERT IN THE GARAGE. WHY DO YOU THINK I ORDERED YOU CHAMPAGNE?
AND JACKY CORE?
I'VE GOT FRIENDS FROM CHICAGO WHO ARE GOING TO PAY HER A LITTLE VISIT.
NO WAY!
THE SOLUTION IS TO MAKE THE SEX FARM, NOT TO TAKE ON THIS MADWOMAN!
JACKY CORE IS RUNNING FOR GOVERNOR. IF SHE IS ELECTED IN TEN DAYS, YOUR BUDDIES FROM CHICAGO WILL LOOK REALLY SMART COMING UP AGAINST HER...
...WE CAN'T LET THIS NUTCASE STOMP ON OUR FREEDOM!
IT'S A QUESTION OF PRINCIPLE!
LEW, WE'RE IN THE PORNO BIZ! DON'T TALK TO ME ABOUT "PRINCIPLES" AND "FREEDOM!"
I LOST A FORTUNE ON THE SEX FARM, FOXY DOESN'T WANT TO PLAY IN IT ANYMORE AND HALF OF THE CAST IS IN THE HOSPITAL. OKAY?
TRY TO SEND JACKY CORE SIX FEET UNDER AND YOU'LL MAKE A MARTYR OUT OF HER AND YOU'LL FIND YOURSELF FACING A TRIAL, WHICH WILL LEAVE YOU EITHER BROKE OR IN AN ELECTRIC CHAIR.
FINISH THE SEX FARM, AND I GUARANTEE YOU A CONTROVERSY THAT WILL BE THE BIGGEST PUBLICITY CAMPAIGN YOU'VE EVER SEEN...AND A MOUNTAIN OF DOUGH!
WAITING FOR THE DOUGH FROM THE SEX FARM GOT ME A BLACK EYE MORE THAN ANYTHING ELSE...AND IT COULD HAVE BEEN WORSE. SURE, I'M A RISK TAKER. SURE, I HATE THESE BASTARDS. BUT I'M ALSO A KID'S MOM...
CONTROVERSY... CONTROVERSY...
AND THIS KID NEEDS HIS MOM TO WORK TO PAY THE RENT, DOESN'T HE? YOU HAVE TO DO THE SEX FARM, FOXY, IT'S NOT JUST THE CASH AT STAKE...
...IT'S OUR CIVIL LIBERTIES THAT ARE BEING THREATENED!

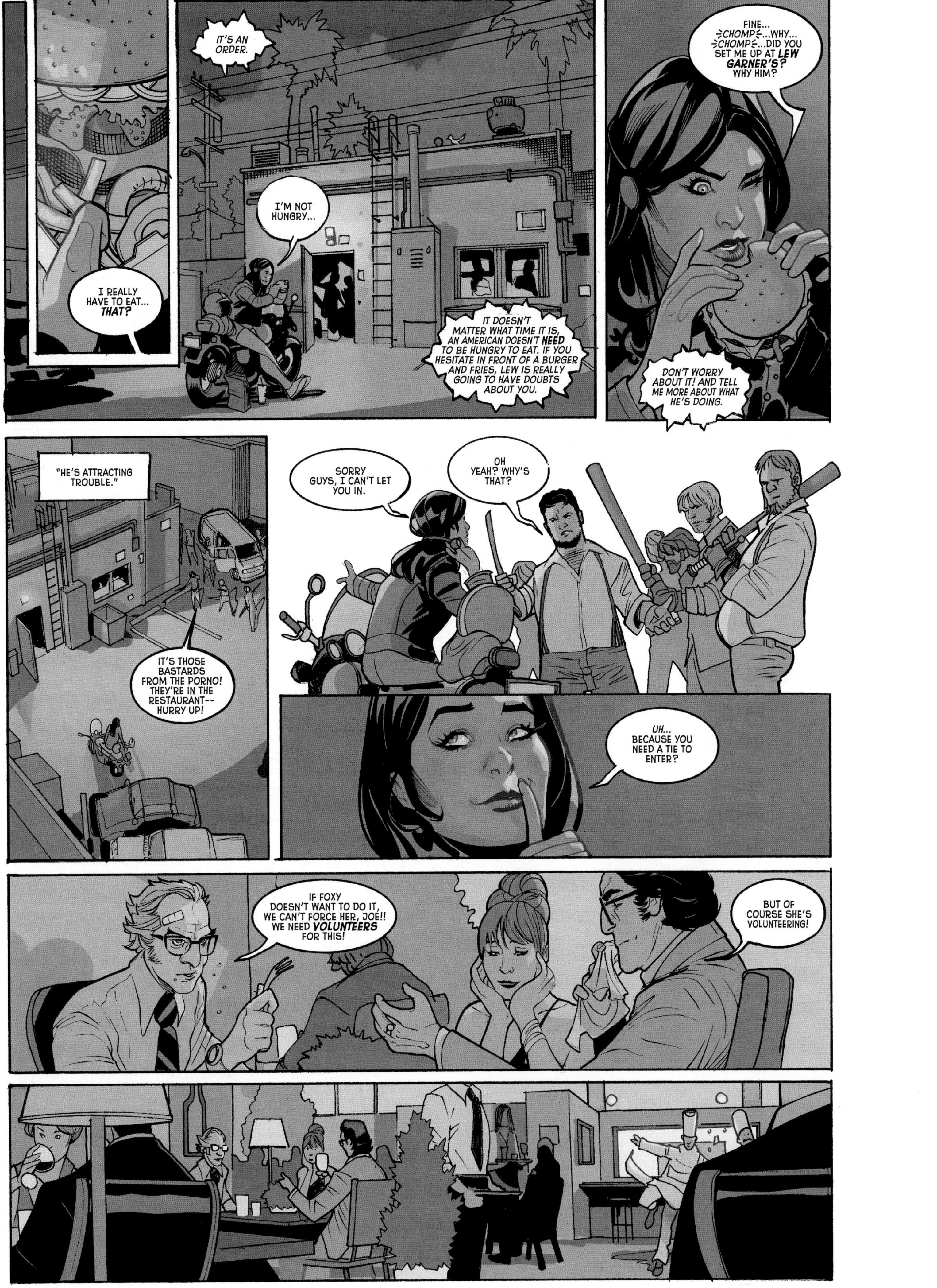
I REALLY HAVE TO EAT... THAT?
IT'S AN ORDER.
I'M NOT HUNGRY...
IT DOESN'T MATTER WHAT TIME IT IS, AN AMERICAN DOESN'T NEED TO BE HUNGRY TO EAT. IF YOU HESITATE IN FRONT OF A BURGER AND FRIES, LEW IS REALLY GOING TO HAVE DOUBTS ABOUT YOU.
FINE... CHOMP... WHY... CHOMP... DID YOU SET ME UP AT LEW GARNER'S? WHY HIM?
DON'T WORRY ABOUT IT! AND TELL ME MORE ABOUT WHAT HE'S DOING.
"HE'S ATTRACTING TROUBLE."
IT'S THOSE BASTARDS FROM THE PORNO! THEY'RE IN THE RESTAURANT-- HURRY UP!
SORRY GUYS, I CAN'T LET YOU IN.
OH YEAH? WHY'S THAT?
UH... BECAUSE YOU NEED A TIE TO ENTER?
IF FOXY DOESN'T WANT TO DO IT, WE CAN'T FORCE HER, JOE!! WE NEED VOLUNTEERS FOR THIS!
BUT OF COURSE SHE'S VOLUNTEERING!

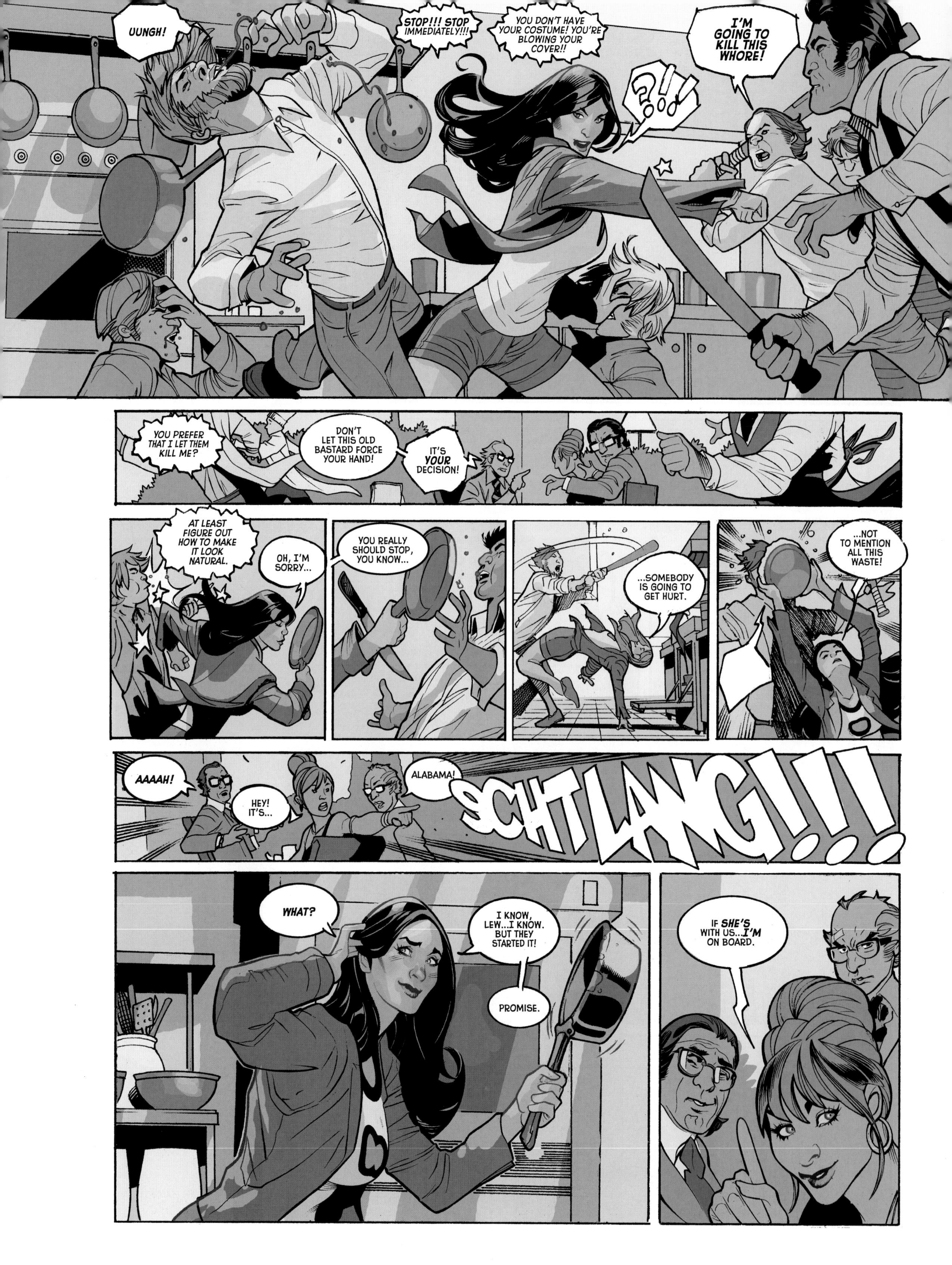
UUNGH!
STOP!!! STOP IMMEDIATELY!!!
YOU DON'T HAVE YOUR COSTUME! YOU'RE BLOWING YOUR COVER!!
?!!
I'M GOING TO KILL THIS WHORE!
YOU PREFER THAT I LET THEM KILL ME?
DON'T LET THIS OLD BASTARD FORCE YOUR HAND!
IT'S YOUR DECISION!
AT LEAST FIGURE OUT HOW TO MAKE IT LOOK NATURAL.
OH, I'M SORRY...
YOU REALLY SHOULD STOP, YOU KNOW...
...SOMEBODY IS GOING TO GET HURT.
...NOT TO MENTION ALL THIS WASTE!
AAAAH!
HEY! IT'S...
ALABAMA!
SCHTLANG!!!
WHAT?
I KNOW, LEW...I KNOW. BUT THEY STARTED IT!
PROMISE.
IF SHE'S WITH US...I'M ON BOARD.

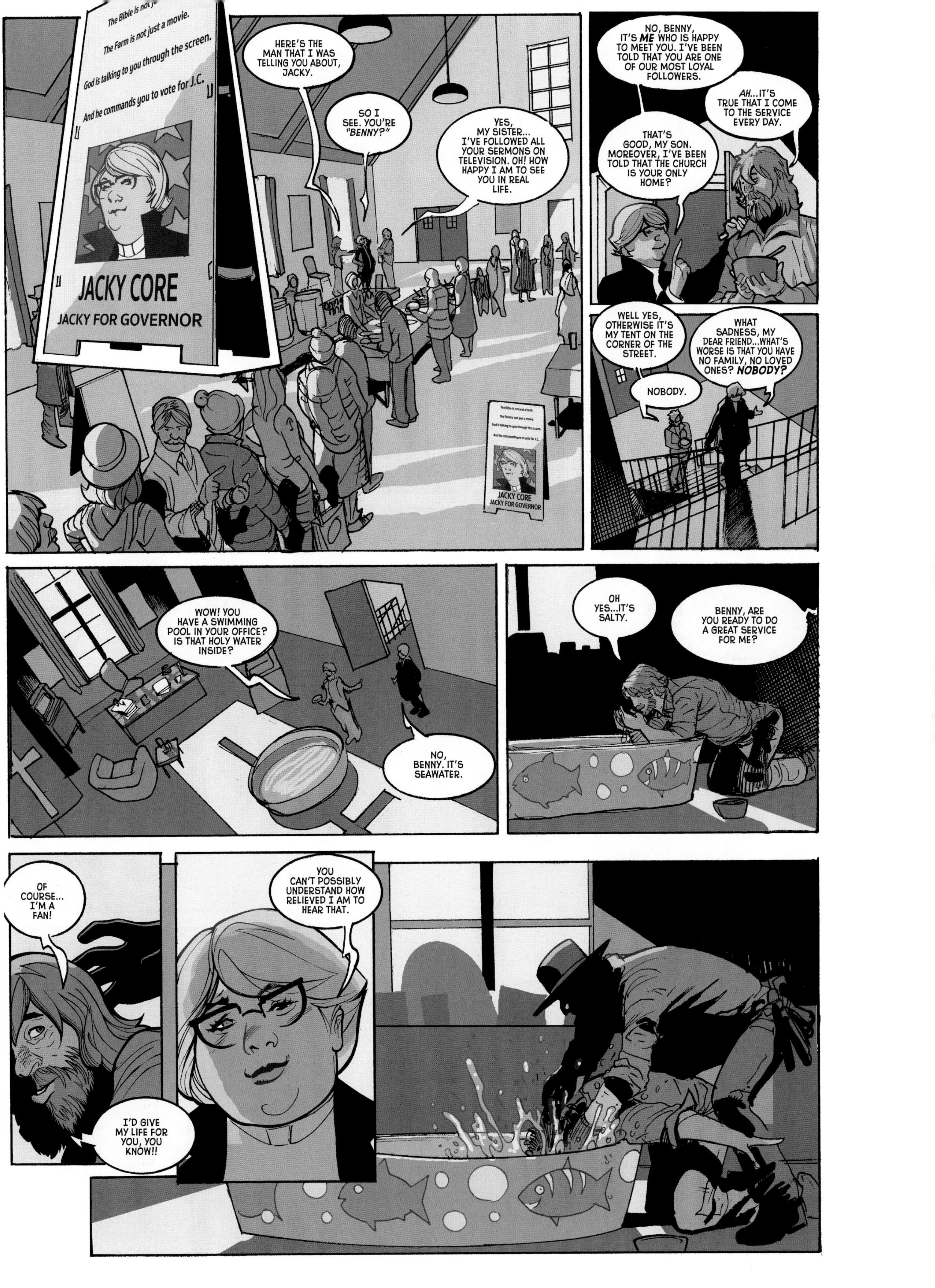
The Bible is not just a book.
The Farm is not just a movie.
God is talking to you through the screen.
And he commands you to vote for J.C.
JACKY CORE
JACKY FOR GOVERNOR
HERE'S THE MAN THAT I WAS TELLING YOU ABOUT, JACKY.
SO I SEE. YOU'RE "BENNY?"
YES, MY SISTER... I'VE FOLLOWED ALL YOUR SERMONS ON TELEVISION. OH! HOW HAPPY I AM TO SEE YOU IN REAL LIFE.
NO, BENNY, IT'S ME WHO IS HAPPY TO MEET YOU. I'VE BEEN TOLD THAT YOU ARE ONE OF OUR MOST LOYAL FOLLOWERS.
AH...IT'S TRUE THAT I COME TO THE SERVICE EVERY DAY.
THAT'S GOOD, MY SON. MOREOVER, I'VE BEEN TOLD THAT THE CHURCH IS YOUR ONLY HOME?
WELL YES, OTHERWISE IT'S MY TENT ON THE CORNER OF THE STREET.
WHAT SADNESS, MY DEAR FRIEND...WHAT'S WORSE IS THAT YOU HAVE NO FAMILY, NO LOVED ONES? NOBODY?
NOBODY.
WOW! YOU HAVE A SWIMMING POOL IN YOUR OFFICE? IS THAT HOLY WATER INSIDE?
NO, BENNY. IT'S SEAWATER.
OH YES...IT'S SALTY.
BENNY, ARE YOU READY TO DO A GREAT SERVICE FOR ME?
OF COURSE... I'M A FAN!
I'D GIVE MY LIFE FOR YOU, YOU KNOW!!
YOU CAN'T POSSIBLY UNDERSTAND HOW RELIEVED I AM TO HEAR THAT.

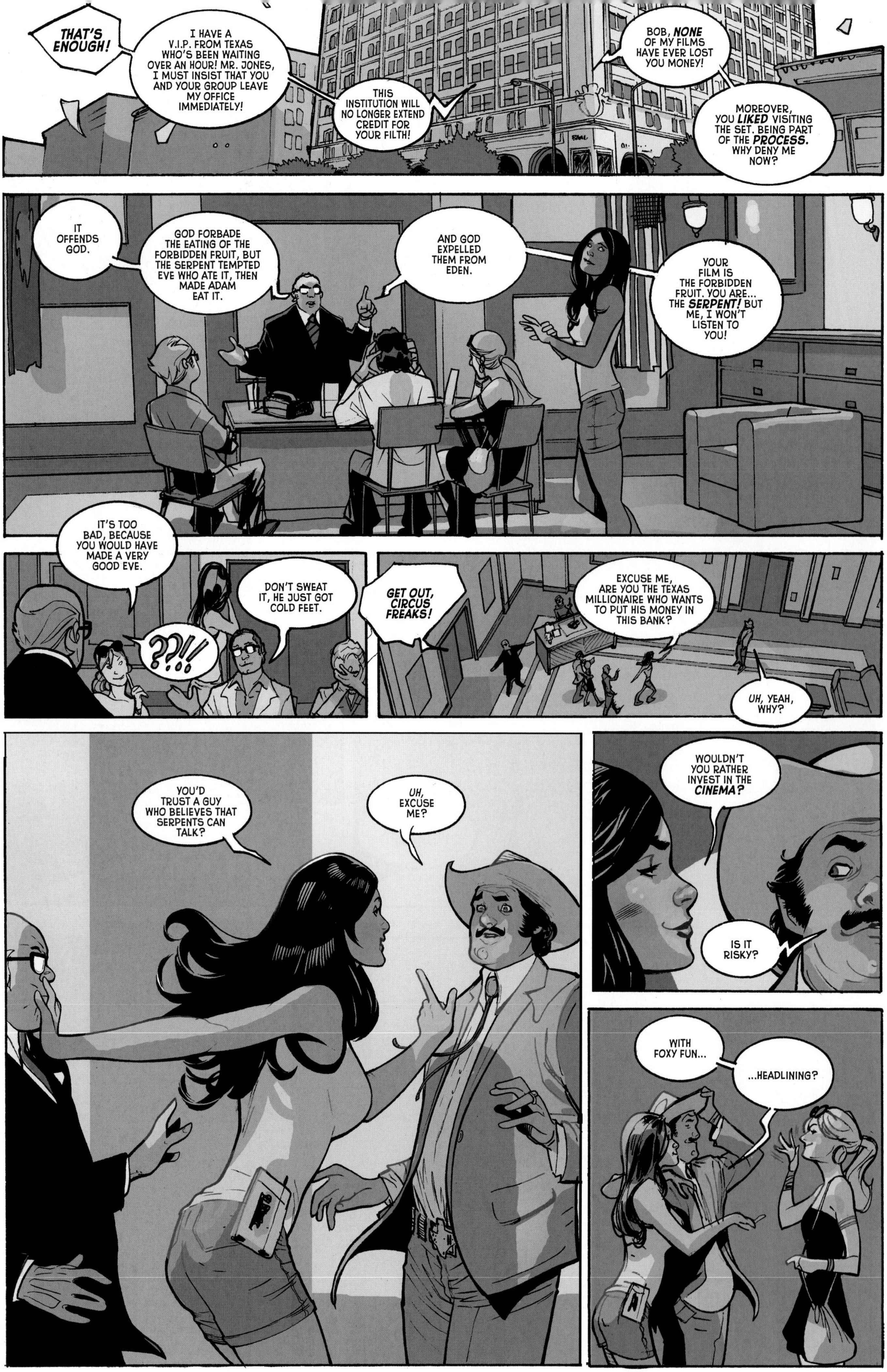

THAT'S ENOUGH!
I HAVE A V.I.P. FROM TEXAS WHO'S BEEN WAITING OVER AN HOUR! MR. JONES, I MUST INSIST THAT YOU AND YOUR GROUP LEAVE MY OFFICE IMMEDIATELY!
THIS INSTITUTION WILL NO LONGER EXTEND CREDIT FOR YOUR FILTH!
BOB, NONE OF MY FILMS HAVE EVER LOST YOU MONEY!
MOREOVER, YOU LIKED VISITING THE SET. BEING PART OF THE PROCESS. WHY DENY ME NOW?
IT OFFENDS GOD.
GOD FORBADE THE EATING OF THE FORBIDDEN FRUIT, BUT THE SERPENT TEMPTED EVE WHO ATE IT, THEN MADE ADAM EAT IT.
AND GOD EXPELLED THEM FROM EDEN.
YOUR FILM IS THE FORBIDDEN FRUIT. YOU ARE... THE SERPENT! BUT ME, I WON'T LISTEN TO YOU!
IT'S TOO BAD, BECAUSE YOU WOULD HAVE MADE A VERY GOOD EVE.
??!!
DON'T SWEAT IT, HE JUST GOT COLD FEET.
GET OUT, CIRCUS FREAKS!
EXCUSE ME, ARE YOU THE TEXAS MILLIONAIRE WHO WANTS TO PUT HIS MONEY IN THIS BANK?
UH, YEAH, WHY?
YOU'D TRUST A GUY WHO BELIEVES THAT SERPENTS CAN TALK?
UH, EXCUSE ME?
WOULDN'T YOU RATHER INVEST IN THE CINEMA?
IS IT RISKY?
WITH FOXY FUN...
...HEADLINING?

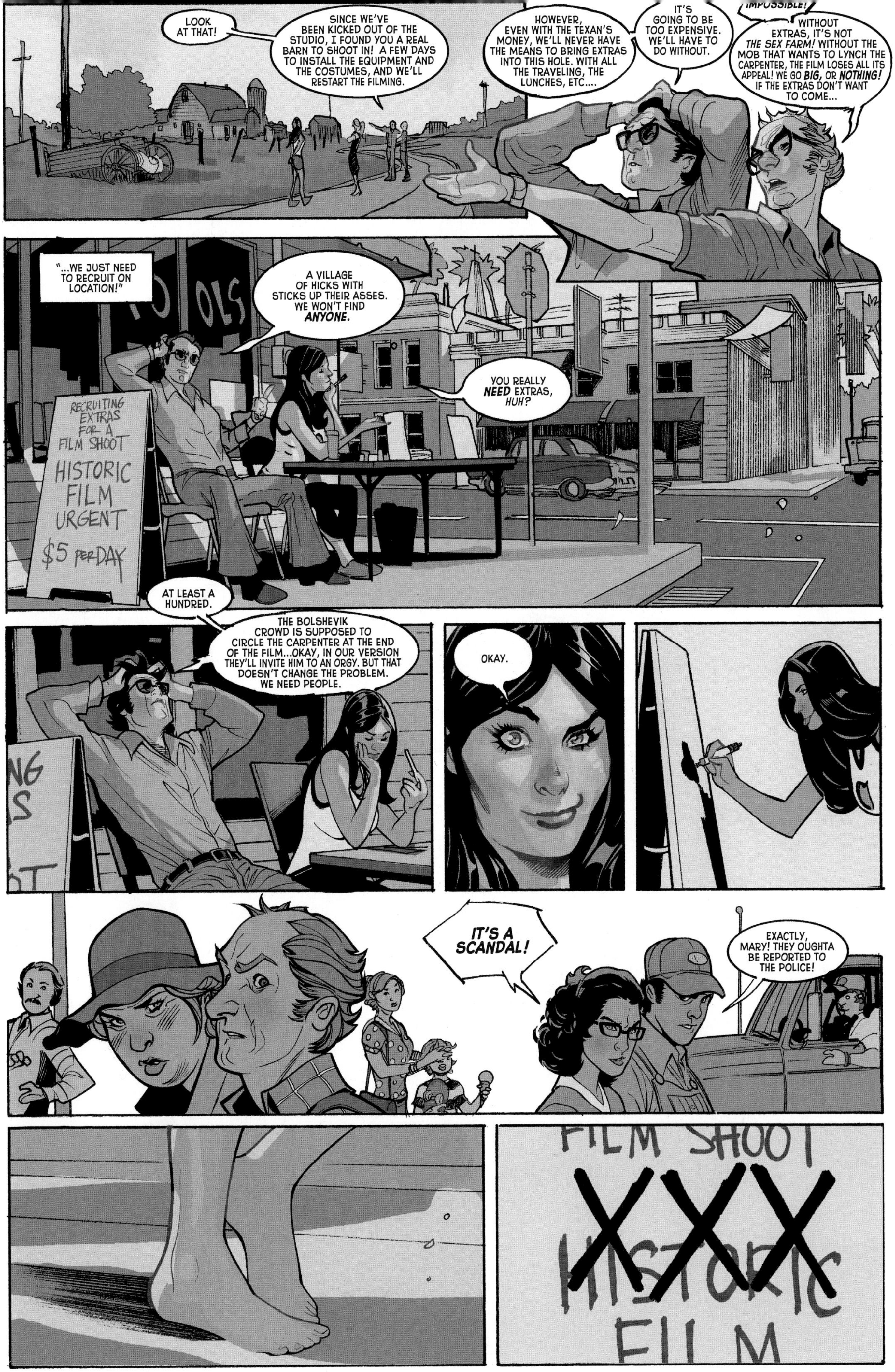
LOOK AT THAT!
SINCE WE'VE BEEN KICKED OUT OF THE STUDIO, I FOUND YOU A REAL BARN TO SHOOT IN! A FEW DAYS TO INSTALL THE EQUIPMENT AND THE COSTUMES, AND WE'LL RESTART THE FILMING.
HOWEVER, EVEN WITH THE TEXAN'S MONEY, WE'LL NEVER HAVE THE MEANS TO BRING EXTRAS INTO THIS HOLE. WITH ALL THE TRAVELING, THE LUNCHES, ETC....
IT'S GOING TO BE TOO EXPENSIVE. WE'LL HAVE TO DO WITHOUT.
IMPOSSIBLE! WITHOUT EXTRAS, IT'S NOT *THE SEX FARM!* WITHOUT THE MOB THAT WANTS TO LYNCH THE CARPENTER, THE FILM LOSES ALL ITS APPEAL! WE GO **BIG,** OR **NOTHING!** IF THE EXTRAS DON'T WANT TO COME...
"...WE JUST NEED TO RECRUIT ON LOCATION!"
A VILLAGE OF HICKS WITH STICKS UP THEIR ASSES. WE WON'T FIND **ANYONE.**
YOU REALLY **NEED** EXTRAS, HUH?
RECRUITING EXTRAS FOR A FILM SHOOT
HISTORIC FILM URGENT
$5 PER DAY
AT LEAST A HUNDRED.
THE BOLSHEVIK CROWD IS SUPPOSED TO CIRCLE THE CARPENTER AT THE END OF THE FILM...OKAY, IN OUR VERSION THEY'LL INVITE HIM TO AN ORGY. BUT THAT DOESN'T CHANGE THE PROBLEM. WE NEED PEOPLE.
OKAY.
IT'S A SCANDAL!
EXACTLY, MARY! THEY OUGHTA BE REPORTED TO THE POLICE!
FILM SHOOT
XXX
HISTORIC
FILM

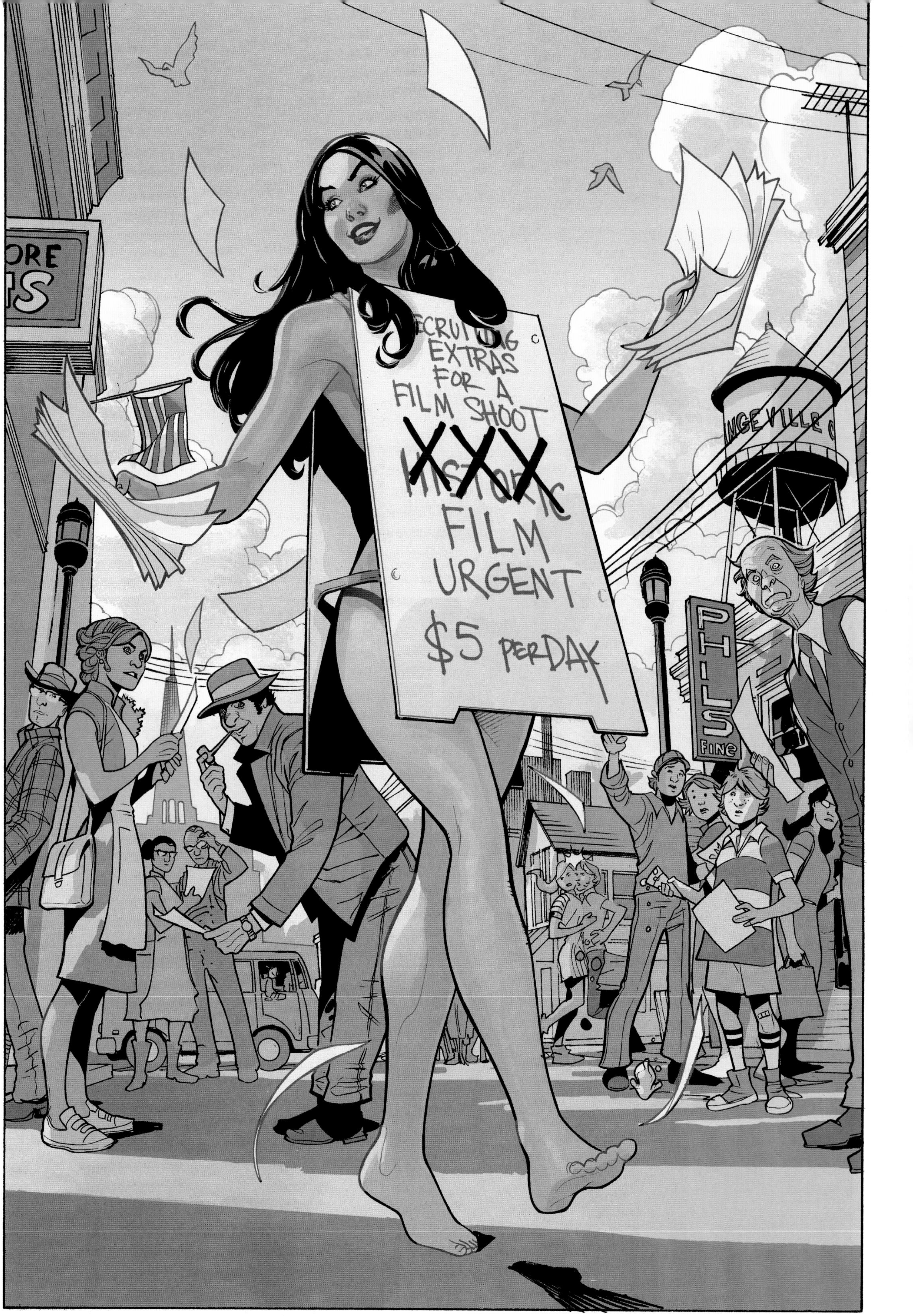

EXTRAS
FOR A
FILM SHOOT
XXX
FILM
URGENT
$5 PER DAY
PHILS
FINE

I'M SORRY, LEW. I MADE EVERYONE *RUN AWAY.* AS SOON AS THEY SAW US, THEY *SCATTERED.*

OH YEAH, WELL THEN I'VE GOT GOOD NEWS...

...THEY'RE BACK.

??????!

WE MAY HAVE FOUND EXTRAS, BUT YOUR LITTLE EXHIBITIONIST ACT COULD HAVE PUT YOU IN JAIL!! SO NOW THAT THE CIRCUS ACTS ARE OVER...

YOU COME TO THE SET TO DROP ME OFF AND PICK ME UP *AND THAT'S ALL!*

I PAY YOU FOR A JOB, I EXPECT IT TO GET DONE!

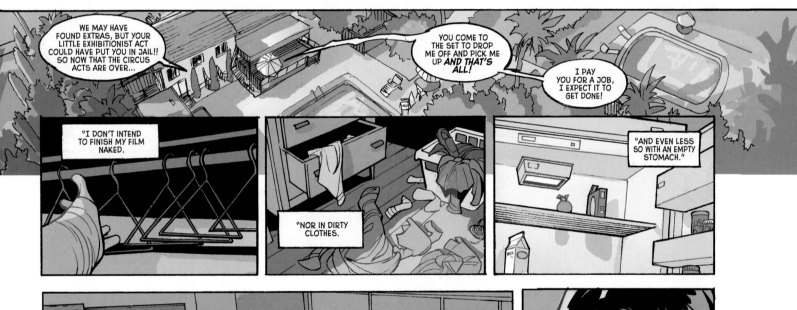

"I DON'T INTEND TO FINISH MY FILM NAKED.

"NOR IN DIRTY CLOTHES.

"AND EVEN LESS SO WITH AN EMPTY STOMACH."

I NEED TO BE 100 PERCENT DEVOTED TO MY FILM, AND THE ONLY THING I NEED TO KNOW IS I CAN TRUST YOU.

CAN I?

I *PROMISE* YOU, YOU CAN.

TWO DAYS! WE WERE SUPPOSED TO HAVE STARTED THE MISSION TWO DAYS AGO! *FUCK! WHAT WERE YOU UP TO?*

I'M ATTEMPTING TO RESOLVE ONE OF THE BIGGEST *MYSTERIES* OF MANKIND.

WHAT? WHAT MYSTERY?

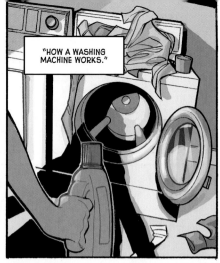

"HOW A WASHING MACHINE WORKS."

ARE YOU *KIDDING* ME?!

I WOULDN'T DARE!

BUT IF YOU DON'T HELP ME, ONE--LEW WILL FIRE ME, TWO--I'LL BREAK MY COVER, AND THREE...I WON'T HAVE ANYTHING LEFT TO WEAR.

THE COPS HAVE THE CARPENTER'S CORPSE, SO FORGET THIS GHOST AND REMEMBER YOUR MISSION... YOU'RE HERE FOR YOUR COUNTRY!

HIS "CORPSE"...?

YOU'RE SURE?

DO I LOOK LIKE I WASH MY CLOTHES MYSELF? JUST LET YOUR THINGS AIR OUT A BIT ON THE WINDOWSILL! THAT'S WHAT I DO!

VERA, YOU NEED TO PULL YOURSELF TOGETHER. GET BACK TO WORK NOW OR THE KGB WILL COME FOR YOU!!

TURN ON THE TELEVISION. YOU KNOW HOW TO DO THAT AT LEAST.

THE BODY OF A MAN WITHOUT IDENTIFICATION BUT CORRESPONDING TO EYEWITNESS DESCRIPTIONS OF THE CARPENTER HAS BEEN FOUND ON A BEACH NEAR SANTA MONICA.

AN INVESTIGATION IS UNDERWAY AND AN ARREST WARRANT HAS BEEN ISSUED FOR THE ONLY SUSPECT...*RED ONE.*

OUR COMMUNITY IS IN MOURNING, THOSE WHO WANT A MORE VIRTUOUS WORLD ARE IN MOURNING, AMERICA IS IN MOURNING...

PRAY FOR THE MEMORY OF HE WHO WE CALL THE CARPENTER, PRAY FOR THE END OF THESE COMMUNISTS AND OF THIS RED ONE WHO HAS KILLED A MAN...

WHEN THE JEWS AND THE ROMANS CRUCIFIED CHRIST, THEY ALSO BELIEVED THAT THEY'D KILLED A MAN...

...AND PERHAPS "MORE" THAN A MAN...

HE WAS THE *SON OF GOD.*

PRAY THAT WE HAVEN'T ALLOWED SUCH A CRIME TO BE COMMITTED AGAIN.

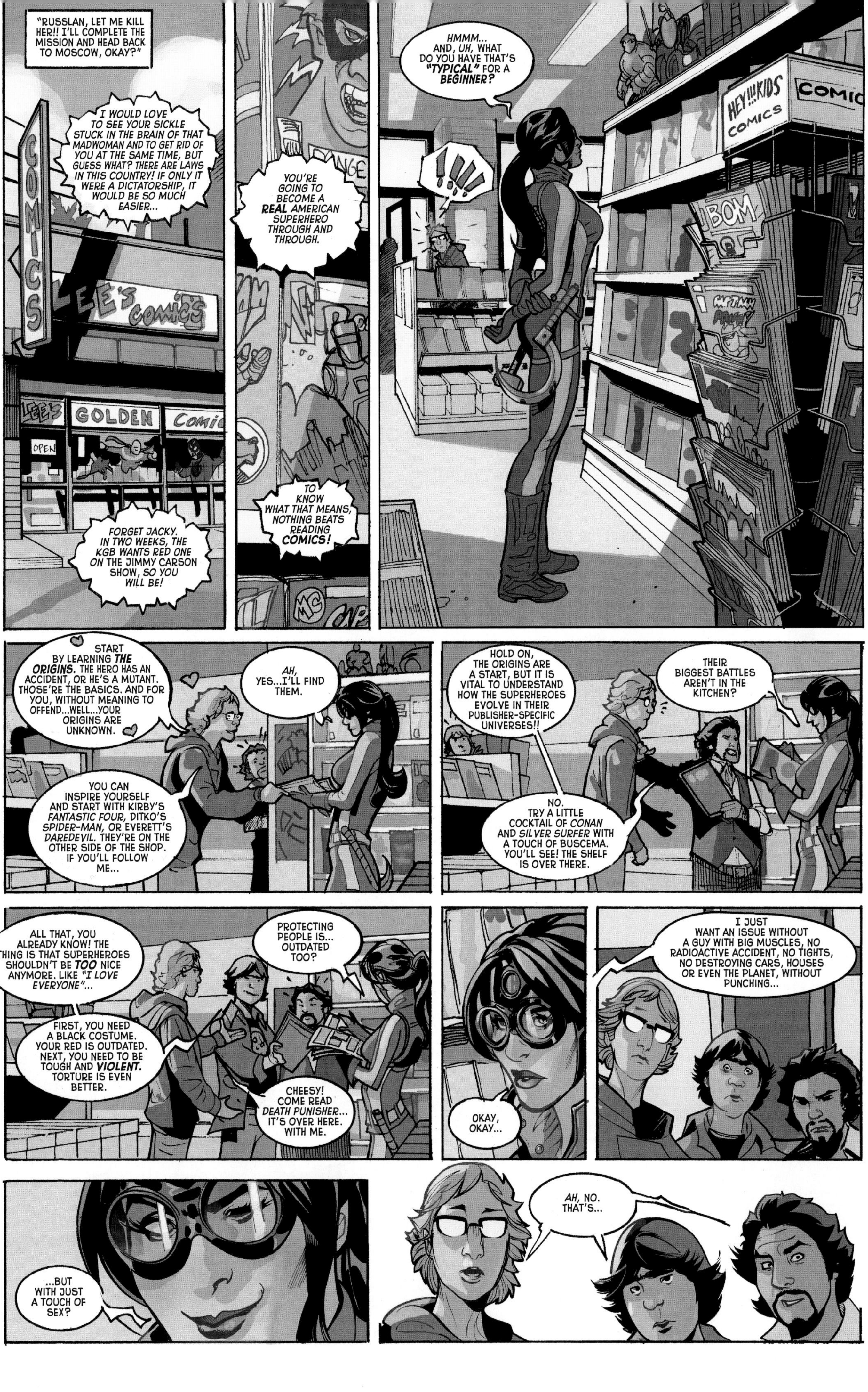
"RUSSLAN, LET ME KILL HER!! I'LL COMPLETE THE MISSION AND HEAD BACK TO MOSCOW, OKAY?"
I WOULD LOVE TO SEE YOUR SICKLE STUCK IN THE BRAIN OF THAT MADWOMAN AND TO GET RID OF YOU AT THE SAME TIME, BUT GUESS WHAT? THERE ARE LAWS IN THIS COUNTRY! IF ONLY IT WERE A DICTATORSHIP, IT WOULD BE SO MUCH EASIER...
COMICS
LEE'S COMICS
LEE'S GOLDEN COMICS
OPEN
FORGET JACKY. IN TWO WEEKS, THE KGB WANTS RED ONE ON THE JIMMY CARSON SHOW, SO YOU WILL BE!
YOU'RE GOING TO BECOME A REAL AMERICAN SUPERHERO THROUGH AND THROUGH.
TO KNOW WHAT THAT MEANS, NOTHING BEATS READING COMICS!
HMMM... AND, UH, WHAT DO YOU HAVE THAT'S "TYPICAL" FOR A BEGINNER?
!!!
HEY!!! KIDS COMICS
COMICS
BOM
START BY LEARNING THE ORIGINS. THE HERO HAS AN ACCIDENT, OR HE'S A MUTANT. THOSE'RE THE BASICS. AND FOR YOU, WITHOUT MEANING TO OFFEND...WELL...YOUR ORIGINS ARE UNKNOWN.
AH, YES...I'LL FIND THEM.
YOU CAN INSPIRE YOURSELF AND START WITH KIRBY'S FANTASTIC FOUR, DITKO'S SPIDER-MAN, OR EVERETT'S DAREDEVIL. THEY'RE ON THE OTHER SIDE OF THE SHOP. IF YOU'LL FOLLOW ME...
HOLD ON, THE ORIGINS ARE A START, BUT IT IS VITAL TO UNDERSTAND HOW THE SUPERHEROES EVOLVE IN THEIR PUBLISHER-SPECIFIC UNIVERSES!!
THEIR BIGGEST BATTLES AREN'T IN THE KITCHEN?
NO. TRY A LITTLE COCKTAIL OF CONAN AND SILVER SURFER WITH A TOUCH OF BUSCEMA. YOU'LL SEE! THE SHELF IS OVER THERE.
ALL THAT, YOU ALREADY KNOW! THE THING IS THAT SUPERHEROES SHOULDN'T BE TOO NICE ANYMORE. LIKE "I LOVE EVERYONE"...
PROTECTING PEOPLE IS... OUTDATED TOO?
FIRST, YOU NEED A BLACK COSTUME. YOUR RED IS OUTDATED. NEXT, YOU NEED TO BE TOUGH AND VIOLENT. TORTURE IS EVEN BETTER.
CHEESY! COME READ DEATH PUNISHER... IT'S OVER HERE. WITH ME.
OKAY, OKAY...
I JUST WANT AN ISSUE WITHOUT A GUY WITH BIG MUSCLES, NO RADIOACTIVE ACCIDENT, NO TIGHTS, NO DESTROYING CARS, HOUSES OR EVEN THE PLANET, WITHOUT PUNCHING...
...BUT WITH JUST A TOUCH OF SEX?
AH, NO. THAT'S...

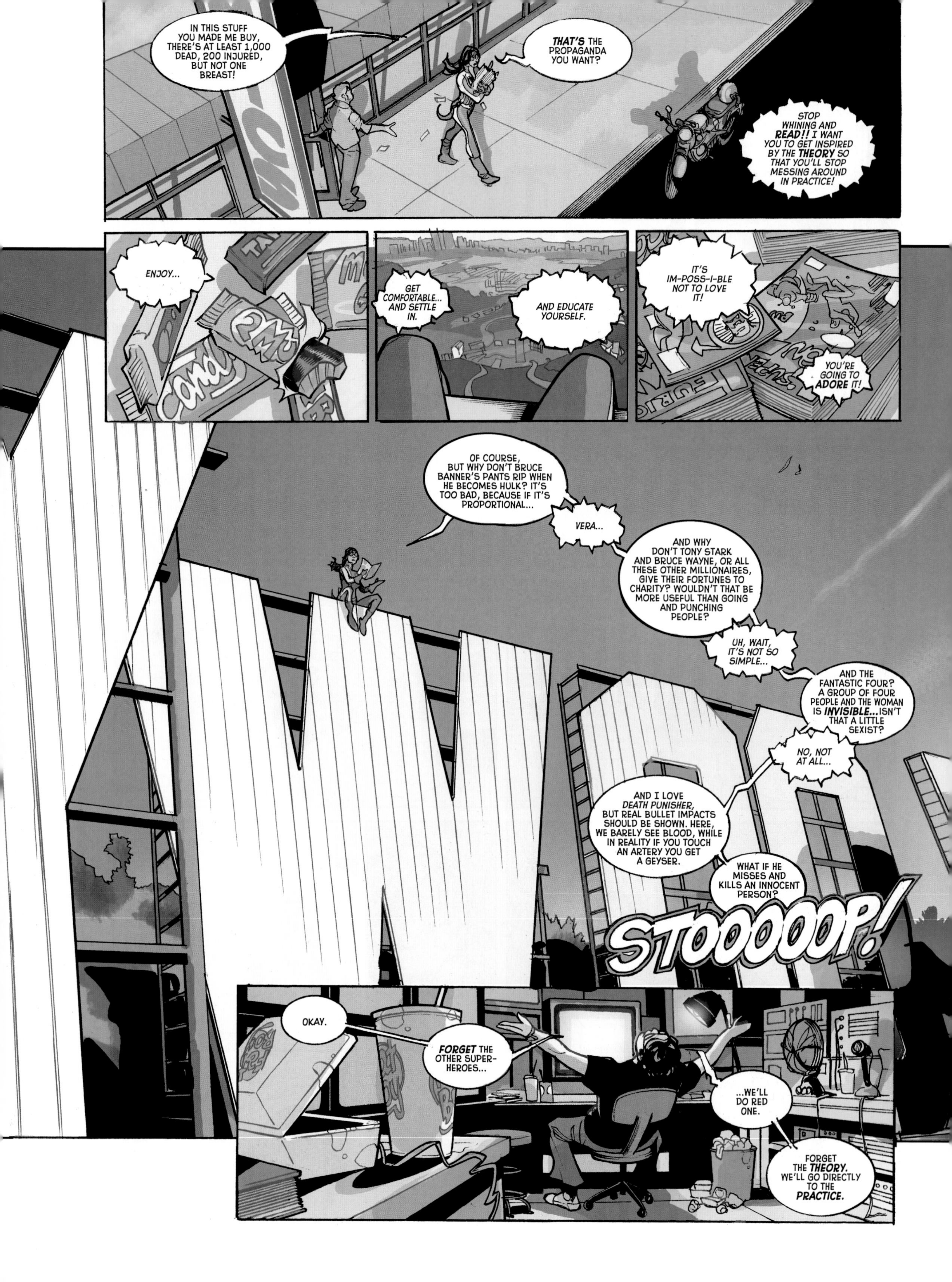

IN THIS STUFF YOU MADE ME BUY, THERE'S AT LEAST 1,000 DEAD, 200 INJURED, BUT NOT ONE BREAST!
THAT'S THE PROPAGANDA YOU WANT?
STOP WHINING AND READ!! I WANT YOU TO GET INSPIRED BY THE THEORY SO THAT YOU'LL STOP MESSING AROUND IN PRACTICE!
ENJOY...
GET COMFORTABLE... AND SETTLE IN.
AND EDUCATE YOURSELF.
IT'S IM-POSS-I-BLE NOT TO LOVE IT!
YOU'RE GOING TO ADORE IT!
OF COURSE, BUT WHY DON'T BRUCE BANNER'S PANTS RIP WHEN HE BECOMES HULK? IT'S TOO BAD, BECAUSE IF IT'S PROPORTIONAL...
VERA...
AND WHY DON'T TONY STARK AND BRUCE WAYNE, OR ALL THESE OTHER MILLIONAIRES, GIVE THEIR FORTUNES TO CHARITY? WOULDN'T THAT BE MORE USEFUL THAN GOING AND PUNCHING PEOPLE?
UH, WAIT, IT'S NOT SO SIMPLE...
AND THE FANTASTIC FOUR? A GROUP OF FOUR PEOPLE AND THE WOMAN IS INVISIBLE... ISN'T THAT A LITTLE SEXIST?
NO, NOT AT ALL...
AND I LOVE DEATH PUNISHER, BUT REAL BULLET IMPACTS SHOULD BE SHOWN. HERE, WE BARELY SEE BLOOD, WHILE IN REALITY IF YOU TOUCH AN ARTERY YOU GET A GEYSER.
WHAT IF HE MISSES AND KILLS AN INNOCENT PERSON?
STOOOOOP!
OKAY.
FORGET THE OTHER SUPER-HEROES...
...WE'LL DO RED ONE.
FORGET THE THEORY. WE'LL GO DIRECTLY TO THE PRACTICE.

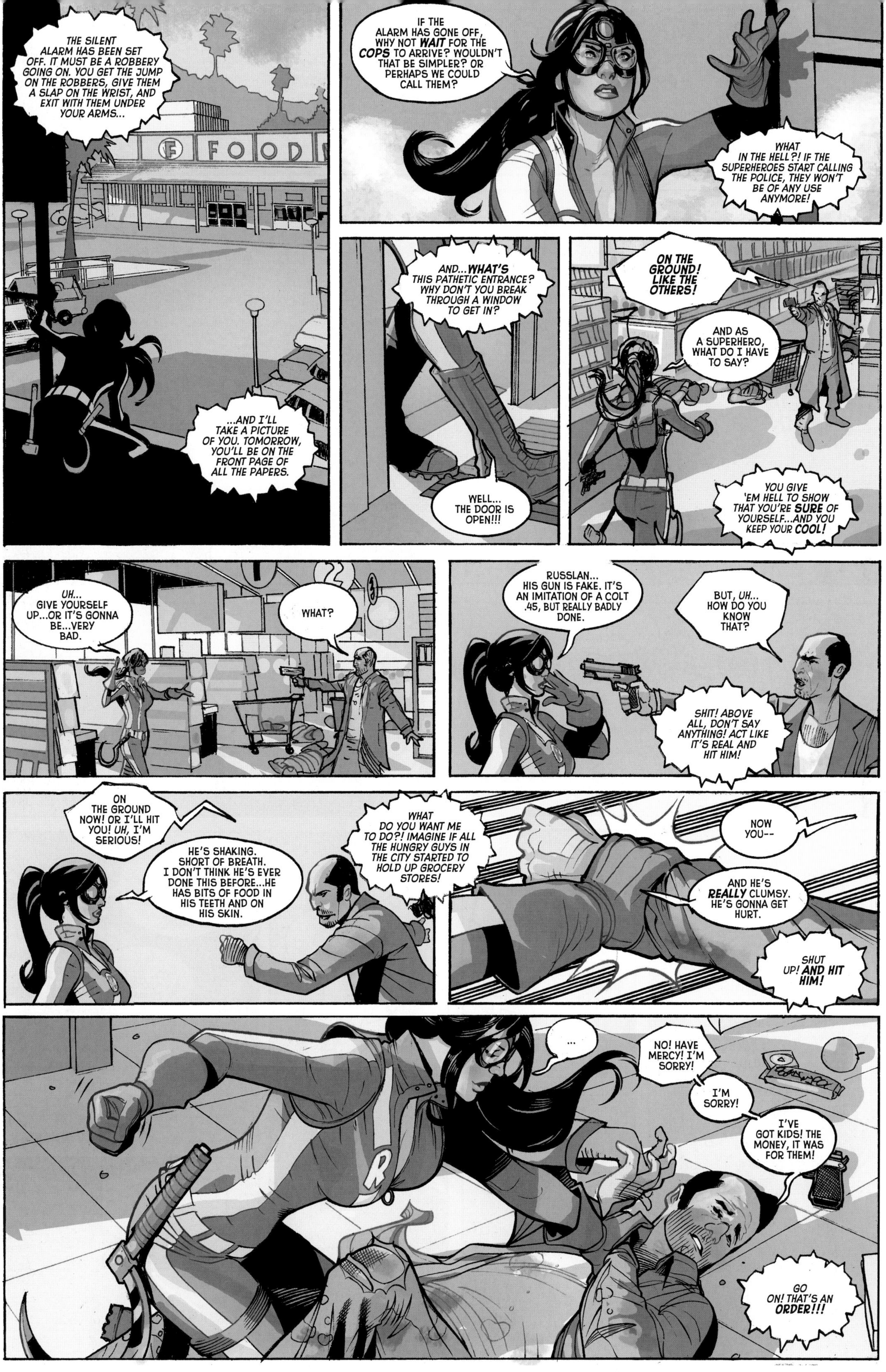
THE SILENT ALARM HAS BEEN SET OFF. IT MUST BE A ROBBERY GOING ON. YOU GET THE JUMP ON THE ROBBERS, GIVE THEM A SLAP ON THE WRIST, AND EXIT WITH THEM UNDER YOUR ARMS...
FOOD
...AND I'LL TAKE A PICTURE OF YOU. TOMORROW, YOU'LL BE ON THE FRONT PAGE OF ALL THE PAPERS.
IF THE ALARM HAS GONE OFF, WHY NOT WAIT FOR THE COPS TO ARRIVE? WOULDN'T THAT BE SIMPLER? OR PERHAPS WE COULD CALL THEM?
WHAT IN THE HELL?! IF THE SUPERHEROES START CALLING THE POLICE, THEY WON'T BE OF ANY USE ANYMORE!
AND...WHAT'S THIS PATHETIC ENTRANCE? WHY DON'T YOU BREAK THROUGH A WINDOW TO GET IN?
WELL... THE DOOR IS OPEN!!!
ON THE GROUND! LIKE THE OTHERS!
AND AS A SUPERHERO, WHAT DO I HAVE TO SAY?
YOU GIVE 'EM HELL TO SHOW THAT YOU'RE SURE OF YOURSELF...AND YOU KEEP YOUR COOL!
UH... GIVE YOURSELF UP...OR IT'S GONNA BE...VERY BAD.
WHAT?
RUSSLAN... HIS GUN IS FAKE. IT'S AN IMITATION OF A COLT .45, BUT REALLY BADLY DONE.
BUT, UH... HOW DO YOU KNOW THAT?
SHIT! ABOVE ALL, DON'T SAY ANYTHING! ACT LIKE IT'S REAL AND HIT HIM!
ON THE GROUND NOW! OR I'LL HIT YOU! UH, I'M SERIOUS!
HE'S SHAKING. SHORT OF BREATH. I DON'T THINK HE'S EVER DONE THIS BEFORE...HE HAS BITS OF FOOD IN HIS TEETH AND ON HIS SKIN.
WHAT DO YOU WANT ME TO DO?! IMAGINE IF ALL THE HUNGRY GUYS IN THE CITY STARTED TO HOLD UP GROCERY STORES!
NOW YOU--
AND HE'S REALLY CLUMSY. HE'S GONNA GET HURT.
SHUT UP! AND HIT HIM!
...
NO! HAVE MERCY! I'M SORRY!
I'M SORRY!
I'VE GOT KIDS! THE MONEY, IT WAS FOR THEM!
GO ON! THAT'S AN ORDER!!!

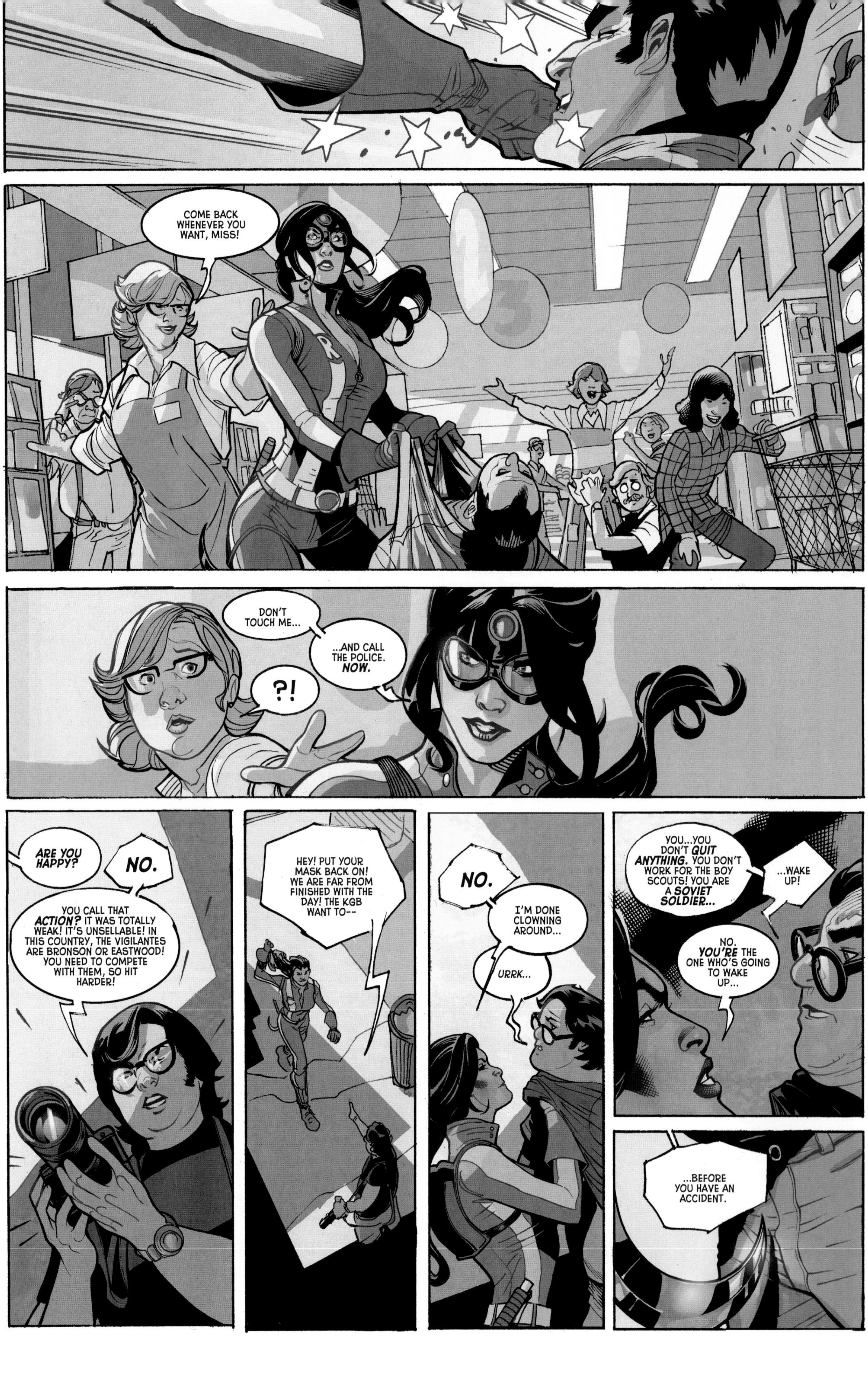
COME BACK WHENEVER YOU WANT, MISS!
DON'T TOUCH ME...
...AND CALL THE POLICE. NOW.
?!
ARE YOU HAPPY?
NO.
YOU CALL THAT ACTION? IT WAS TOTALLY WEAK! IT'S UNSELLABLE! IN THIS COUNTRY, THE VIGILANTES ARE BRONSON OR EASTWOOD! YOU NEED TO COMPETE WITH THEM, SO HIT HARDER!
HEY! PUT YOUR MASK BACK ON! WE ARE FAR FROM FINISHED WITH THE DAY! THE KGB WANT TO--
NO.
I'M DONE CLOWNING AROUND...
URRK...
YOU...YOU DON'T QUIT ANYTHING. YOU DON'T WORK FOR THE BOY SCOUTS! YOU ARE A SOVIET SOLDIER...
...WAKE UP!
NO. YOU'RE THE ONE WHO'S GOING TO WAKE UP...
...BEFORE YOU HAVE AN ACCIDENT.

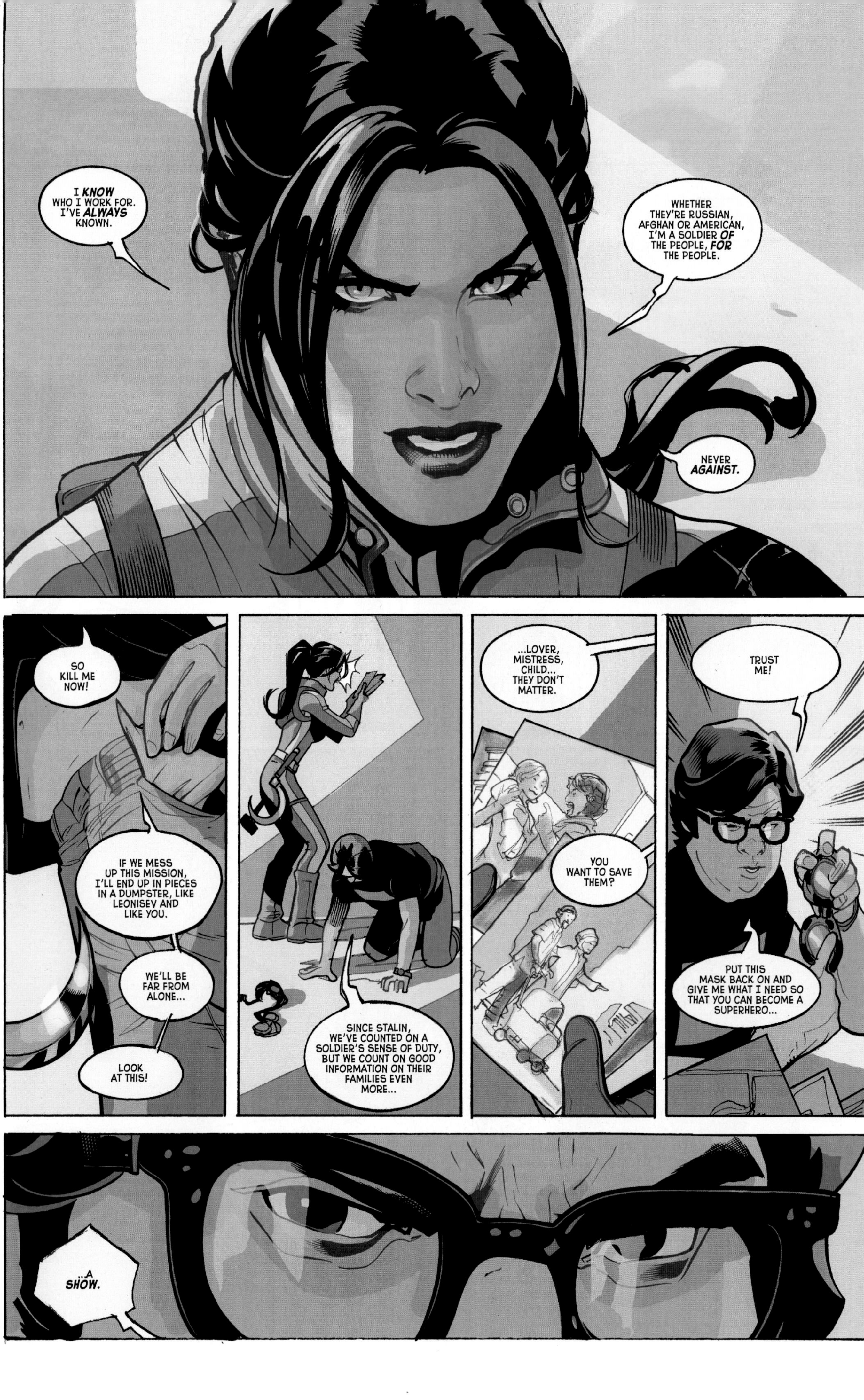

I KNOW WHO I WORK FOR. I'VE ALWAYS KNOWN.
WHETHER THEY'RE RUSSIAN, AFGHAN OR AMERICAN, I'M A SOLDIER OF THE PEOPLE, FOR THE PEOPLE.
NEVER AGAINST.
SO KILL ME NOW!
IF WE MESS UP THIS MISSION, I'LL END UP IN PIECES IN A DUMPSTER, LIKE LEONISEV AND LIKE YOU.
WE'LL BE FAR FROM ALONE...
LOOK AT THIS!
SINCE STALIN, WE'VE COUNTED ON A SOLDIER'S SENSE OF DUTY, BUT WE COUNT ON GOOD INFORMATION ON THEIR FAMILIES EVEN MORE...
...LOVER, MISTRESS, CHILD... THEY DON'T MATTER.
YOU WANT TO SAVE THEM?
TRUST ME!
PUT THIS MASK BACK ON AND GIVE ME WHAT I NEED SO THAT YOU CAN BECOME A SUPERHERO...
...A SHOW.

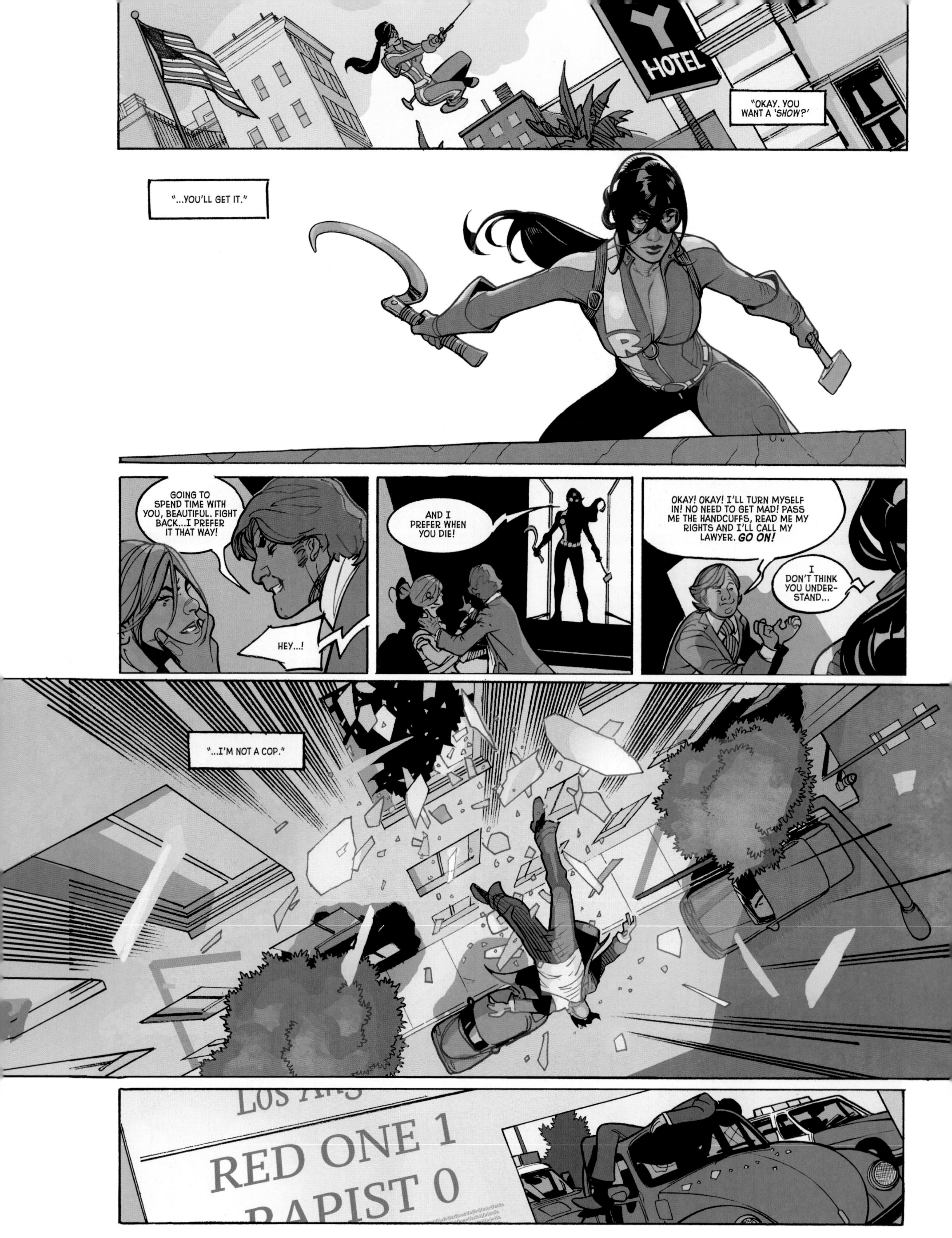

"OKAY. YOU WANT A 'SHOW?'
"...YOU'LL GET IT."
GOING TO SPEND TIME WITH YOU, BEAUTIFUL. FIGHT BACK...I PREFER IT THAT WAY!
HEY...!
AND I PREFER WHEN YOU DIE!
OKAY! OKAY! I'LL TURN MYSELF IN! NO NEED TO GET MAD! PASS ME THE HANDCUFFS, READ ME MY RIGHTS AND I'LL CALL MY LAWYER. GO ON!
I DON'T THINK YOU UNDER-STAND...
"...I'M NOT A COP."
RED ONE 1
RAPIST 0

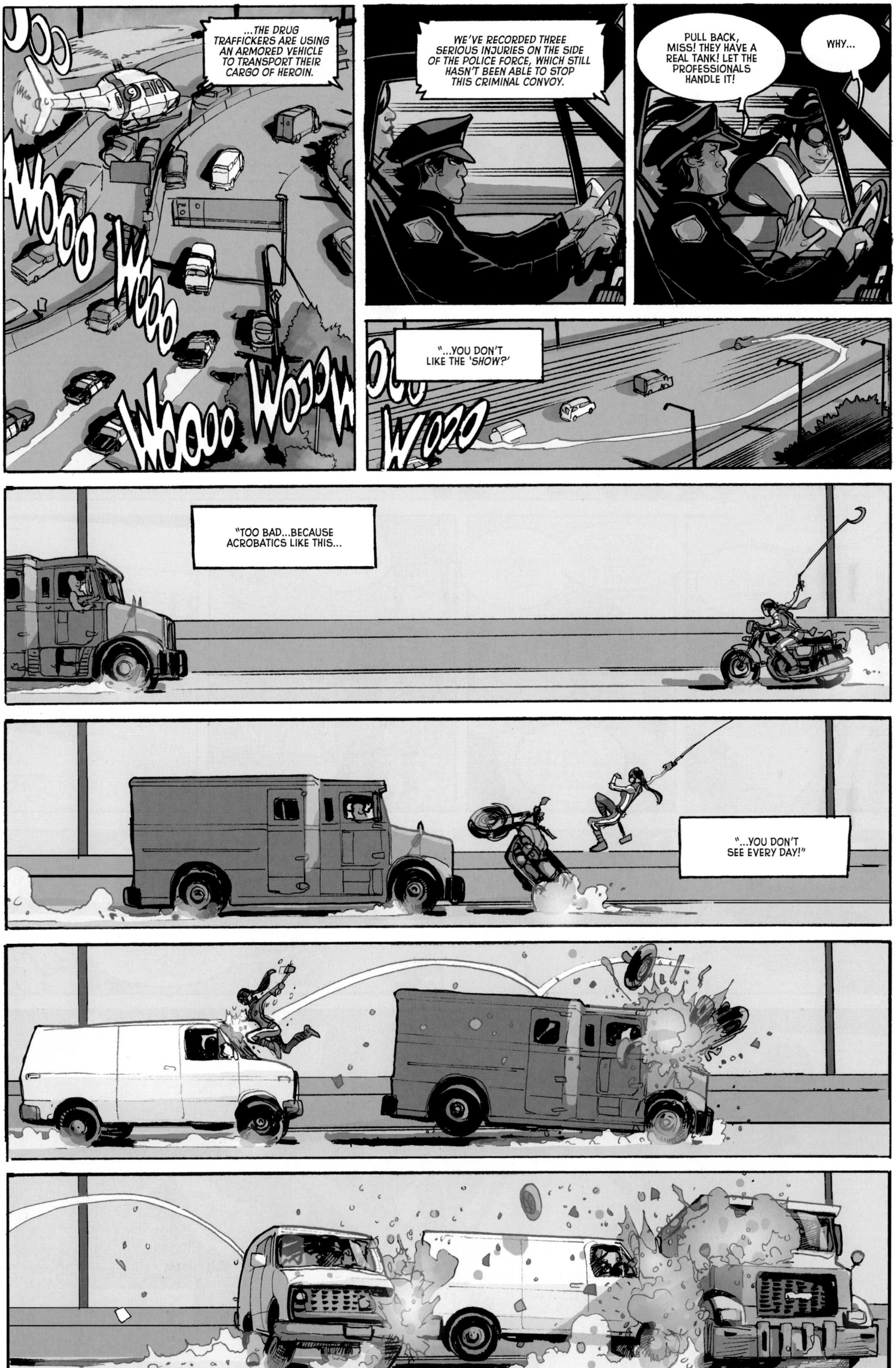
...THE DRUG TRAFFICKERS ARE USING AN ARMORED VEHICLE TO TRANSPORT THEIR CARGO OF HEROIN.
WOOO WOOO WOOO WOOO WOOO
WE'VE RECORDED THREE SERIOUS INJURIES ON THE SIDE OF THE POLICE FORCE, WHICH STILL HASN'T BEEN ABLE TO STOP THIS CRIMINAL CONVOY.
PULL BACK, MISS! THEY HAVE A REAL TANK! LET THE PROFESSIONALS HANDLE IT!
WHY...
"...YOU DON'T LIKE THE 'SHOW?'
"TOO BAD...BECAUSE ACROBATICS LIKE THIS...
"...YOU DON'T SEE EVERY DAY!"

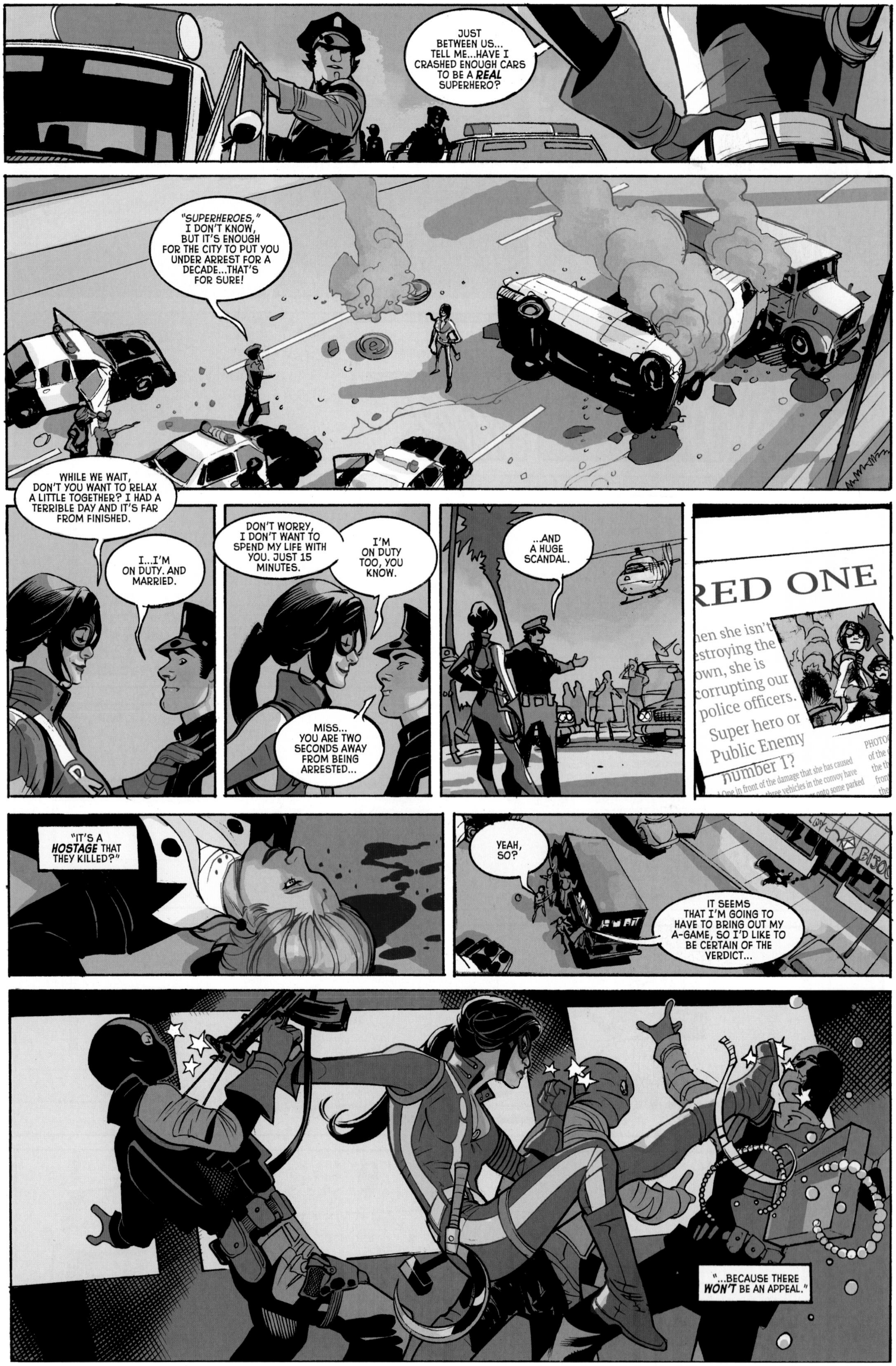
JUST BETWEEN US... TELL ME...HAVE I CRASHED ENOUGH CARS TO BE A *REAL* SUPERHERO?
"*SUPERHEROES,*" I DON'T KNOW, BUT IT'S ENOUGH FOR THE CITY TO PUT YOU UNDER ARREST FOR A DECADE...THAT'S FOR SURE!
WHILE WE WAIT, DON'T YOU WANT TO RELAX A LITTLE TOGETHER? I HAD A TERRIBLE DAY AND IT'S FAR FROM FINISHED.
I...I'M ON DUTY. AND MARRIED.
DON'T WORRY, I DON'T WANT TO SPEND MY LIFE WITH YOU. JUST 15 MINUTES.
I'M ON DUTY TOO, YOU KNOW.
MISS... YOU ARE TWO SECONDS AWAY FROM BEING ARRESTED...
...AND A HUGE SCANDAL.
RED ONE
hen she isn't
estroying the
own, she is
corrupting our
police officers.
Super hero or
Public Enemy
number 1?
"IT'S A *HOSTAGE* THAT THEY KILLED?"
YEAH, SO?
IT SEEMS THAT I'M GOING TO HAVE TO BRING OUT MY A-GAME, SO I'D LIKE TO BE CERTAIN OF THE VERDICT...
"...BECAUSE THERE *WON'T* BE AN APPEAL."

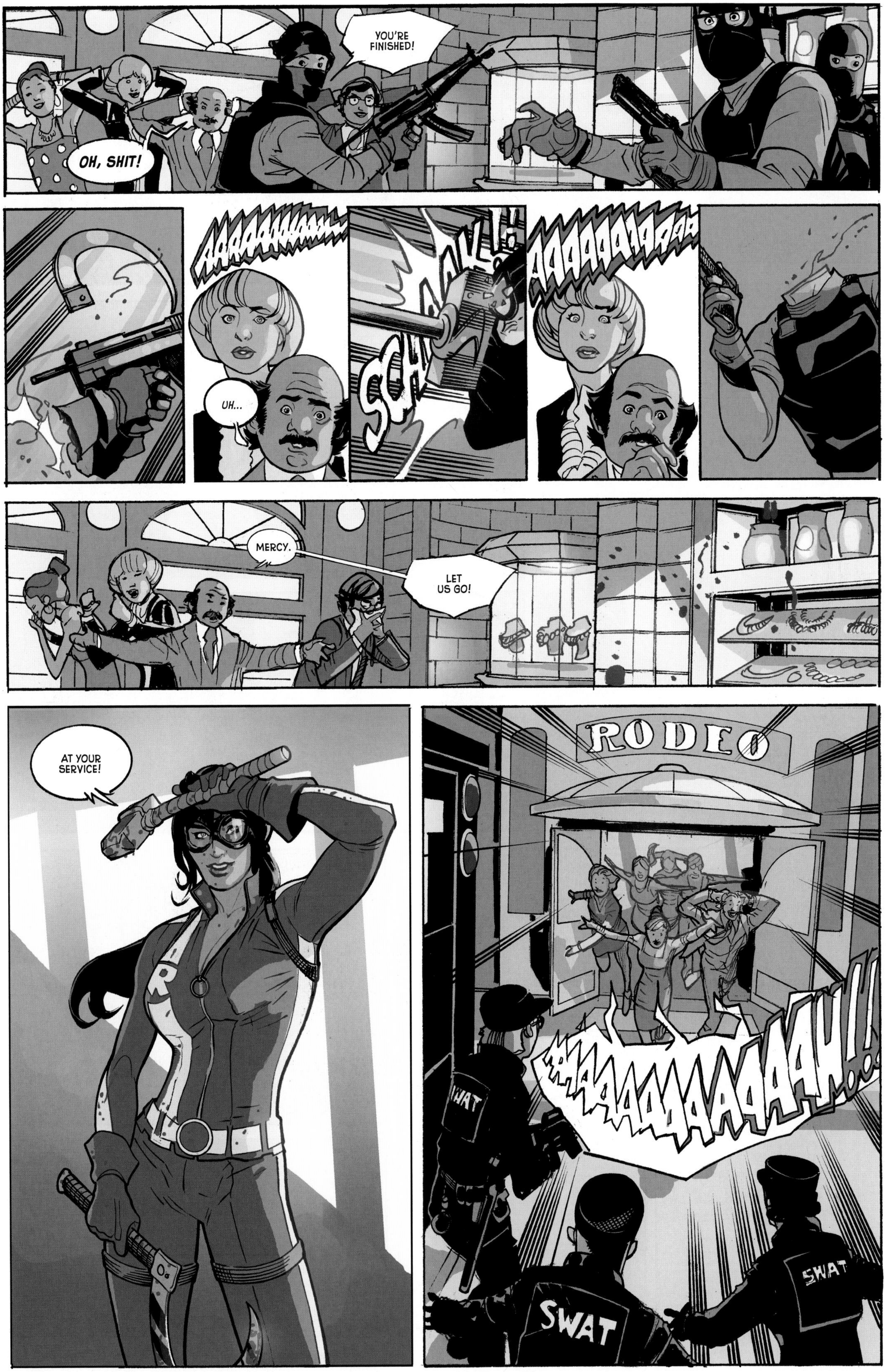

YOU'RE FINISHED!
OH, SHIT!
UH...
MERCY.
LET US GO!
AT YOUR SERVICE!
RODEO
SWAT
SWAT
SWAT

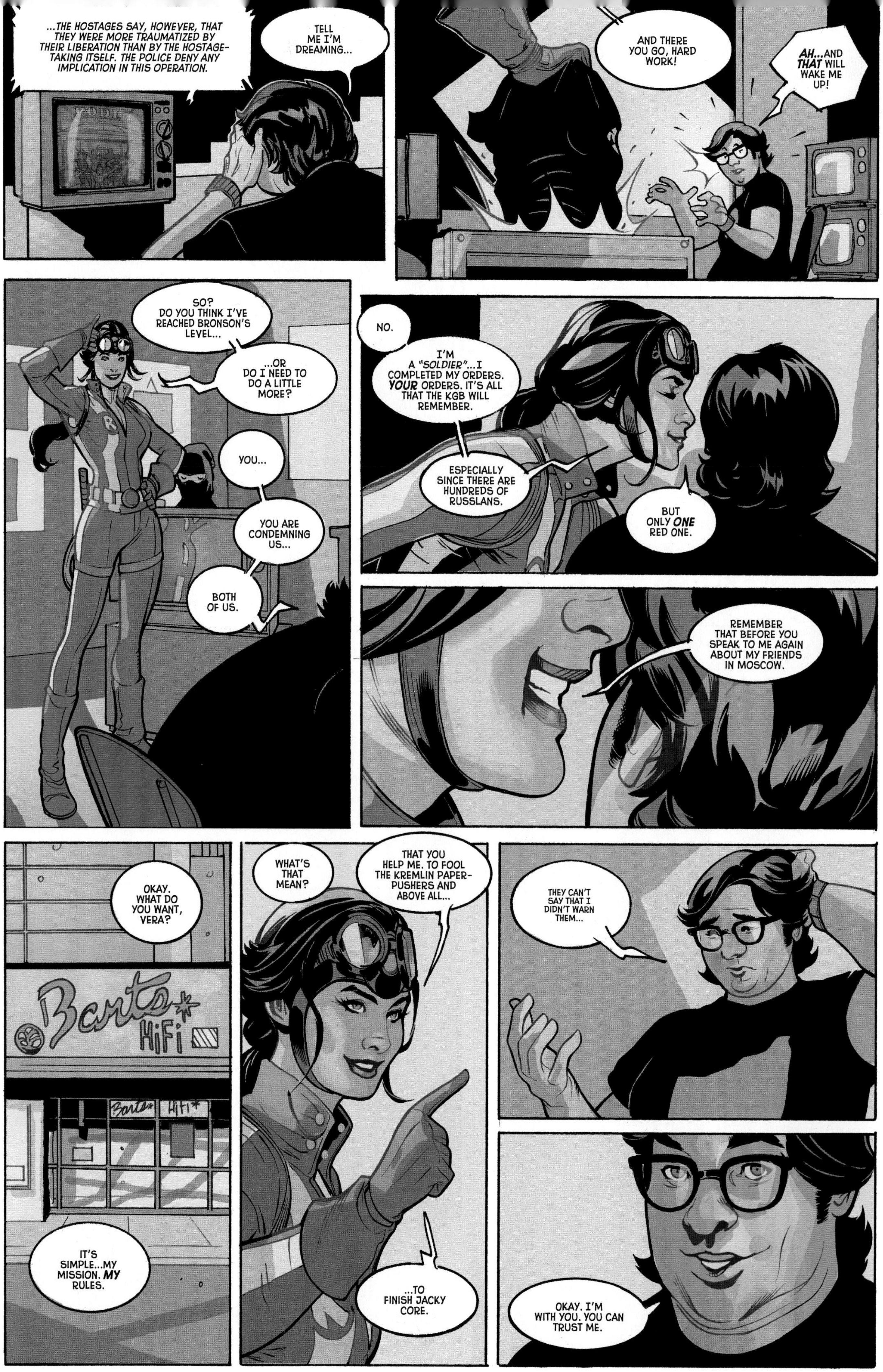
...THE HOSTAGES SAY, HOWEVER, THAT THEY WERE MORE TRAUMATIZED BY THEIR LIBERATION THAN BY THE HOSTAGE-TAKING ITSELF. THE POLICE DENY ANY IMPLICATION IN THIS OPERATION.
TELL ME I'M DREAMING...
AND THERE YOU GO, HARD WORK!
AH...AND THAT WILL WAKE ME UP!
SO? DO YOU THINK I'VE REACHED BRONSON'S LEVEL...
...OR DO I NEED TO DO A LITTLE MORE?
YOU...
YOU ARE CONDEMNING US...
BOTH OF US.
NO.
I'M A "SOLDIER"...I COMPLETED MY ORDERS. YOUR ORDERS. IT'S ALL THAT THE KGB WILL REMEMBER.
ESPECIALLY SINCE THERE ARE HUNDREDS OF RUSSIANS.
BUT ONLY ONE RED ONE.
REMEMBER THAT BEFORE YOU SPEAK TO ME AGAIN ABOUT MY FRIENDS IN MOSCOW.
OKAY. WHAT DO YOU WANT, VERA?
Barts HiFi
IT'S SIMPLE...MY MISSION. MY RULES.
WHAT'S THAT MEAN?
THAT YOU HELP ME. TO FOOL THE KREMLIN PAPER-PUSHERS AND ABOVE ALL...
...TO FINISH JACKY CORE.
THEY CAN'T SAY THAT I DIDN'T WARN THEM...
OKAY. I'M WITH YOU. YOU CAN TRUST ME.

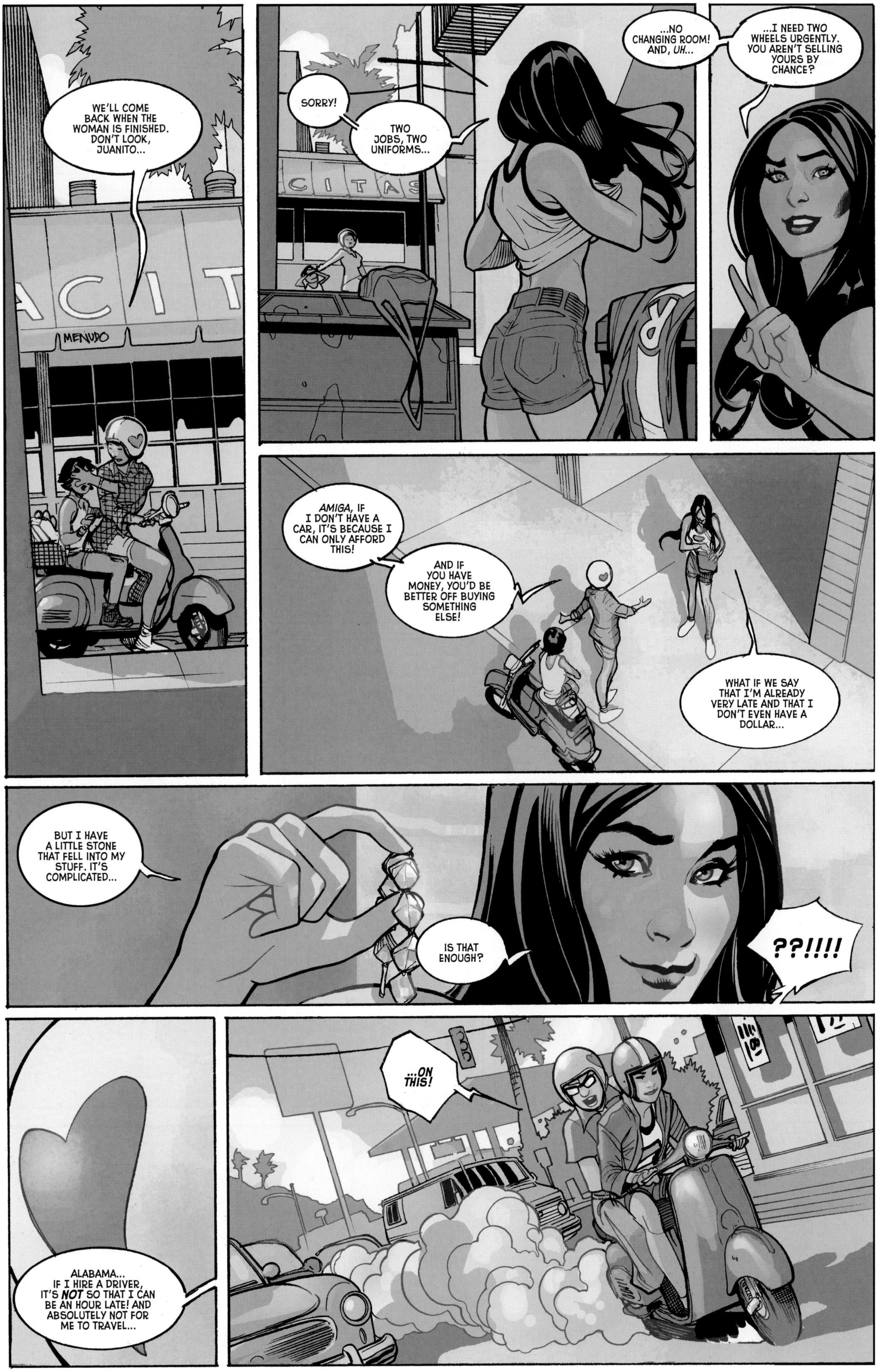
WE'LL COME BACK WHEN THE WOMAN IS FINISHED. DON'T LOOK, JUANITO...
ACIT
MENUDO
CITAS
SORRY!
TWO JOBS, TWO UNIFORMS...
...NO CHANGING ROOM! AND, UH...
...I NEED TWO WHEELS URGENTLY. YOU AREN'T SELLING YOURS BY CHANCE?
AMIGA, IF I DON'T HAVE A CAR, IT'S BECAUSE I CAN ONLY AFFORD THIS!
AND IF YOU HAVE MONEY, YOU'D BE BETTER OFF BUYING SOMETHING ELSE!
WHAT IF WE SAY THAT I'M ALREADY VERY LATE AND THAT I DON'T EVEN HAVE A DOLLAR...
BUT I HAVE A LITTLE STONE THAT FELL INTO MY STUFF. IT'S COMPLICATED...
IS THAT ENOUGH?
??!!!!
ALABAMA... IF I HIRE A DRIVER, IT'S NOT SO THAT I CAN BE AN HOUR LATE! AND ABSOLUTELY NOT FOR ME TO TRAVEL...
...ON THIS!

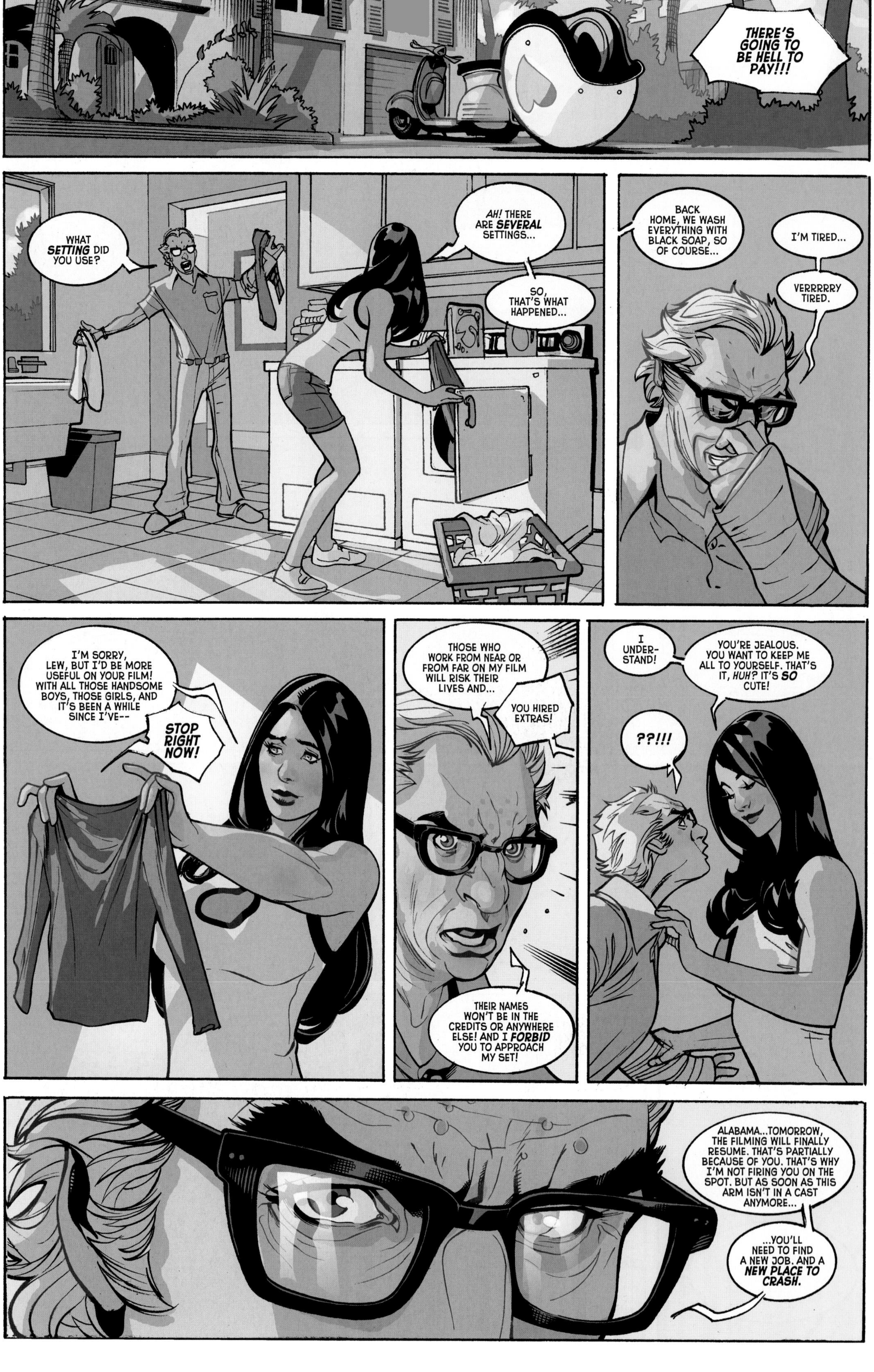
THERE'S GOING TO BE HELL TO PAY!!!
WHAT SETTING DID YOU USE?
AH! THERE ARE SEVERAL SETTINGS...
SO, THAT'S WHAT HAPPENED...
BACK HOME, WE WASH EVERYTHING WITH BLACK SOAP, SO OF COURSE...
I'M TIRED...
VERRRRRY TIRED.
I'M SORRY, LEW, BUT I'D BE MORE USEFUL ON YOUR FILM! WITH ALL THOSE HANDSOME BOYS, THOSE GIRLS, AND IT'S BEEN A WHILE SINCE I'VE--
STOP RIGHT NOW!
THOSE WHO WORK FROM NEAR OR FROM FAR ON MY FILM WILL RISK THEIR LIVES AND...
YOU HIRED EXTRAS!
THEIR NAMES WON'T BE IN THE CREDITS OR ANYWHERE ELSE! AND I FORBID YOU TO APPROACH MY SET!
I UNDER-STAND!
YOU'RE JEALOUS. YOU WANT TO KEEP ME ALL TO YOURSELF. THAT'S IT, HUH? IT'S SO CUTE!
??!!!
ALABAMA...TOMORROW, THE FILMING WILL FINALLY RESUME. THAT'S PARTIALLY BECAUSE OF YOU. THAT'S WHY I'M NOT FIRING YOU ON THE SPOT. BUT AS SOON AS THIS ARM ISN'T IN A CAST ANYMORE...
...YOU'LL NEED TO FIND A NEW JOB. AND A NEW PLACE TO CRASH.

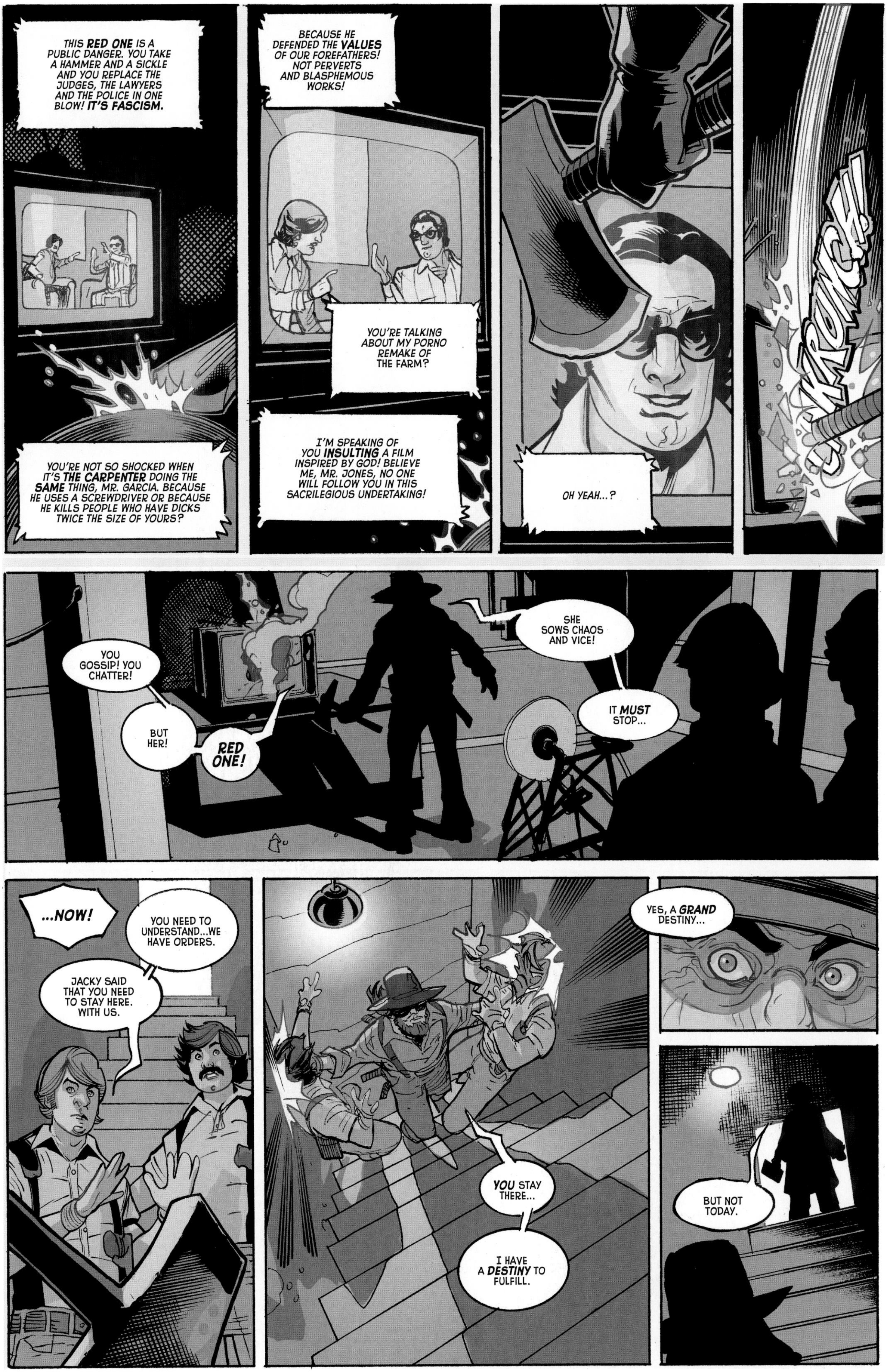
THIS RED ONE IS A PUBLIC DANGER. YOU TAKE A HAMMER AND A SICKLE AND YOU REPLACE THE JUDGES, THE LAWYERS AND THE POLICE IN ONE BLOW! IT'S FASCISM.
YOU'RE NOT SO SHOCKED WHEN IT'S THE CARPENTER DOING THE SAME THING, MR. GARCIA. BECAUSE HE USES A SCREWDRIVER OR BECAUSE HE KILLS PEOPLE WHO HAVE DICKS TWICE THE SIZE OF YOURS?
BECAUSE HE DEFENDED THE VALUES OF OUR FOREFATHERS! NOT PERVERTS AND BLASPHEMOUS WORKS!
YOU'RE TALKING ABOUT MY PORNO REMAKE OF THE FARM?
I'M SPEAKING OF YOU INSULTING A FILM INSPIRED BY GOD! BELIEVE ME, MR. JONES, NO ONE WILL FOLLOW YOU IN THIS SACRILEGIOUS UNDERTAKING!
OH YEAH...?
KRUNCH!
YOU GOSSIP! YOU CHATTER!
BUT HER!
RED ONE!
SHE SOWS CHAOS AND VICE!
IT MUST STOP...
...NOW!
YOU NEED TO UNDERSTAND...WE HAVE ORDERS.
JACKY SAID THAT YOU NEED TO STAY HERE. WITH US.
YOU STAY THERE...
I HAVE A DESTINY TO FULFILL.
YES, A GRAND DESTINY...
BUT NOT TODAY.

THIS WHORE OF SODOM MUST DIE!

NO.

NOT YET...

GIVE ME A REASON!

YOU'RE DEAD.

JESUS STAYED THREE DAYS IN HIS GRAVE BEFORE BEING REVIVED...

HE CAME BACK STRONGER, AND MORE BELOVED, THAN EVER BEFORE.

YOU, TOO, WILL COME BACK TO LIFE, MY LOVE, AND TOGETHER WE'LL PURGE THE WORLD OF THE DEVIL AND HIS COMMUNIST DESCENDANTS.

BUT FIRST, TOMORROW, WE'LL BURY YOU AS IS NECESSARY SO THAT ALL WILL REMEMBER THE LOVE THEY HOLD FOR YOU...

I... I DON'T HAVE THE STRENGTH TO WAIT.

I CRAVE...

AND I AM HERE TO BRING YOU HIS PRESENCE!

"YOU'RE THE CARPENTER, AND GOD ENSURES THAT YOU WILL MISS NEITHER BREAD NOR WINE..."

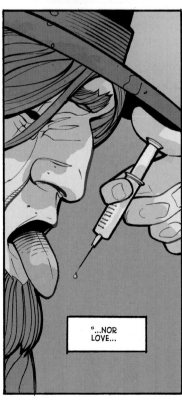

"...NOR LOVE..."

"...NOR FORCE."

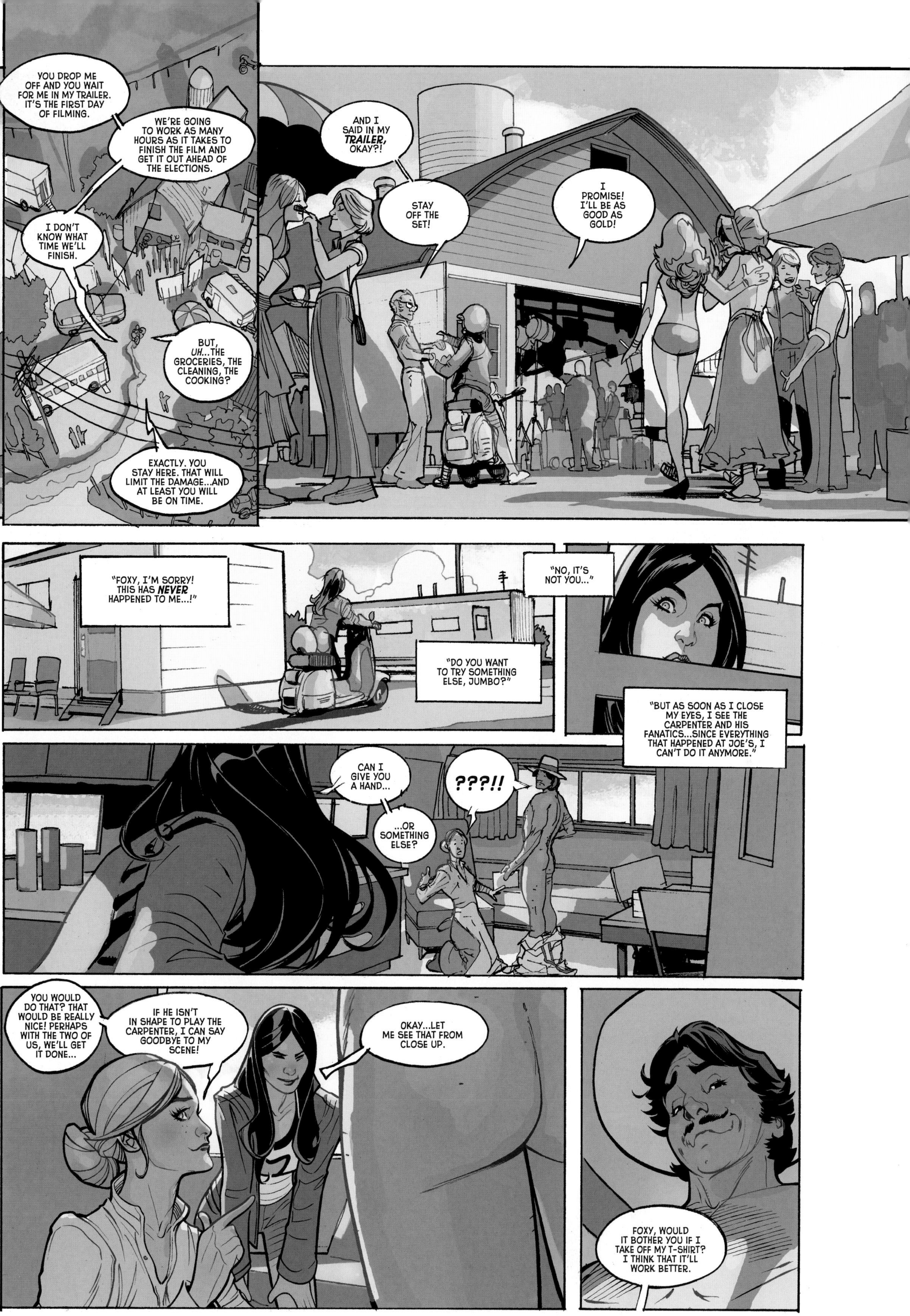
YOU DROP ME OFF AND YOU WAIT FOR ME IN MY TRAILER. IT'S THE FIRST DAY OF FILMING.
WE'RE GOING TO WORK AS MANY HOURS AS IT TAKES TO FINISH THE FILM AND GET IT OUT AHEAD OF THE ELECTIONS.
I DON'T KNOW WHAT TIME WE'LL FINISH.
BUT, *UH*...THE GROCERIES, THE CLEANING, THE COOKING?
EXACTLY. YOU STAY HERE. THAT WILL LIMIT THE DAMAGE...AND AT LEAST YOU WILL BE ON TIME.
AND I SAID IN MY ***TRAILER,*** OKAY?!
STAY OFF THE SET!
I PROMISE! I'LL BE AS GOOD AS GOLD!
"FOXY, I'M SORRY! THIS HAS ***NEVER*** HAPPENED TO ME...!"
"DO YOU WANT TO TRY SOMETHING ELSE, JUMBO?"
"NO, IT'S NOT YOU..."
"BUT AS SOON AS I CLOSE MY EYES, I SEE THE CARPENTER AND HIS FANATICS...SINCE EVERYTHING THAT HAPPENED AT JOE'S, I CAN'T DO IT ANYMORE."
CAN I GIVE YOU A HAND...
...OR SOMETHING ELSE?
???!!
YOU WOULD DO THAT? THAT WOULD BE REALLY NICE! PERHAPS WITH THE TWO OF US, WE'LL GET IT DONE...
IF HE ISN'T IN SHAPE TO PLAY THE CARPENTER, I CAN SAY GOODBYE TO MY SCENE!
OKAY...LET ME SEE THAT FROM CLOSE UP.
FOXY, WOULD IT BOTHER YOU IF I TAKE OFF MY T-SHIRT? I THINK THAT IT'LL WORK BETTER.

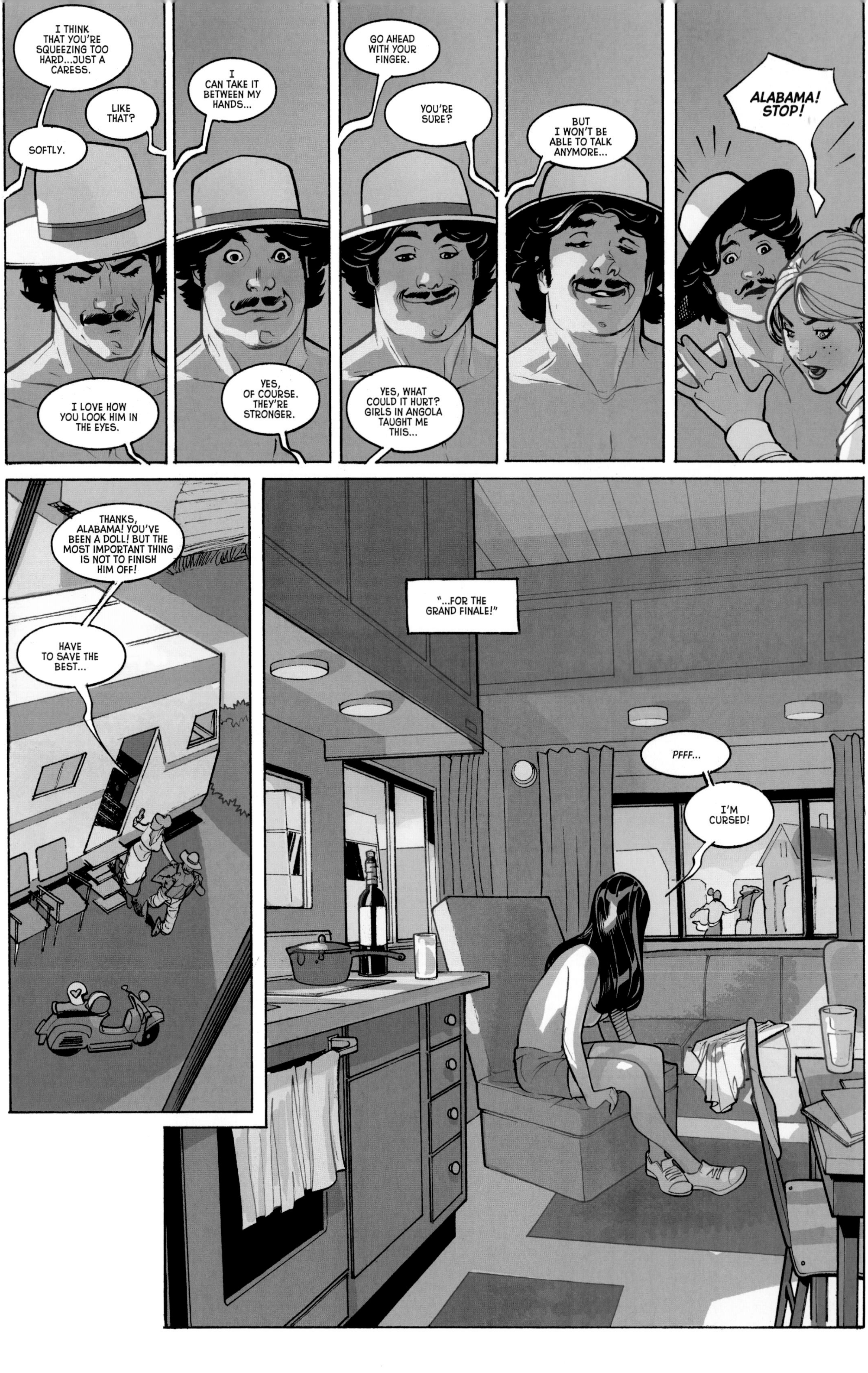
I THINK THAT YOU'RE SQUEEZING TOO HARD...JUST A CARESS.
LIKE THAT?
SOFTLY.
I LOVE HOW YOU LOOK HIM IN THE EYES.
I CAN TAKE IT BETWEEN MY HANDS...
YES, OF COURSE. THEY'RE STRONGER.
GO AHEAD WITH YOUR FINGER.
YOU'RE SURE?
YES, WHAT COULD IT HURT? GIRLS IN ANGOLA TAUGHT ME THIS...
BUT I WON'T BE ABLE TO TALK ANYMORE...
ALABAMA! STOP!
THANKS, ALABAMA! YOU'VE BEEN A DOLL! BUT THE MOST IMPORTANT THING IS NOT TO FINISH HIM OFF!
HAVE TO SAVE THE BEST...
"...FOR THE GRAND FINALE!"
PFFF...
I'M CURSED!

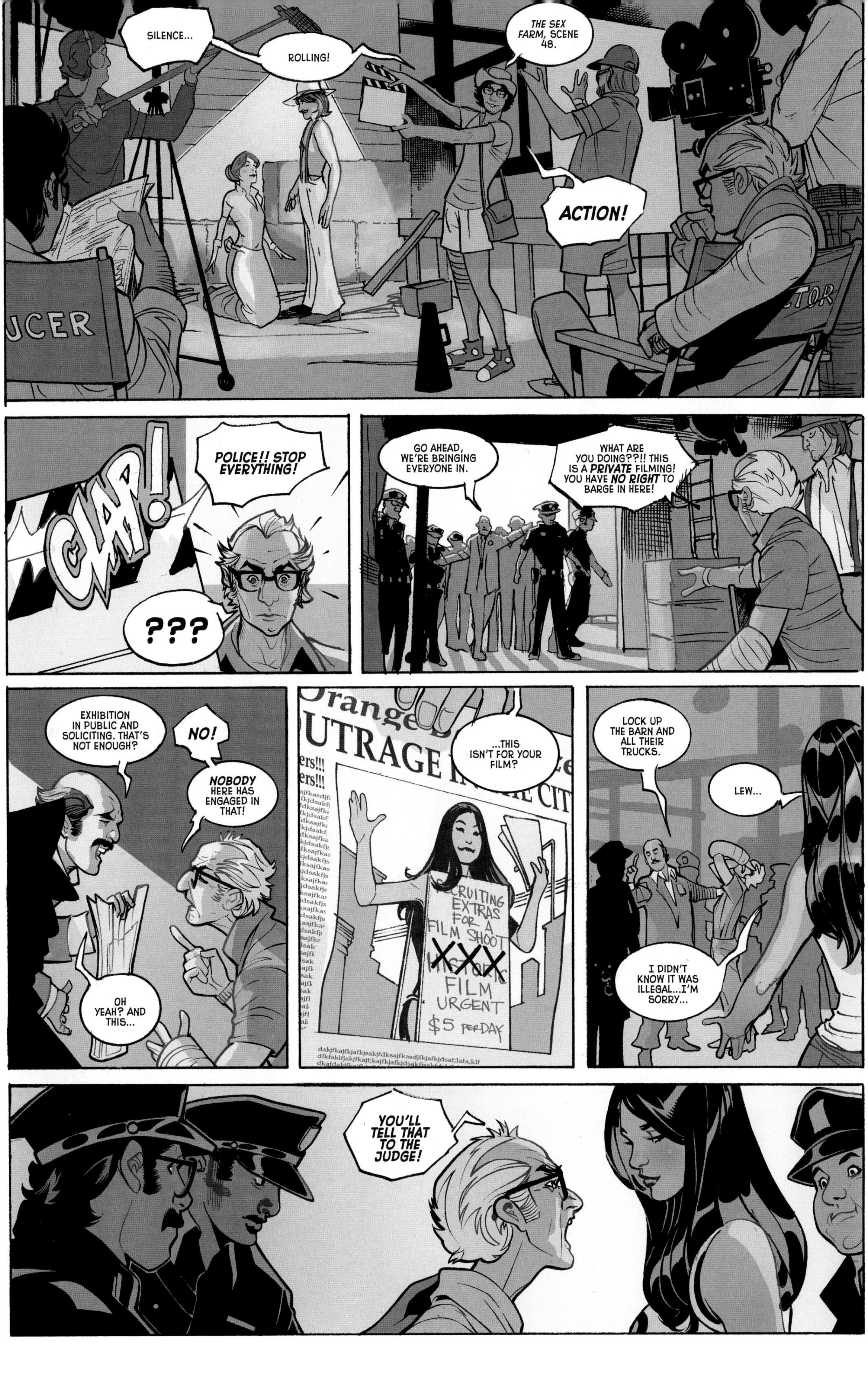
SILENCE...
ROLLING!
THE SEX FARM, SCENE 48.
ACTION!
CLAP!
POLICE!! STOP EVERYTHING!
???
GO AHEAD, WE'RE BRINGING EVERYONE IN.
WHAT ARE YOU DOING??!! THIS IS A ***PRIVATE*** FILMING! YOU HAVE ***NO RIGHT*** TO BARGE IN HERE!
EXHIBITION IN PUBLIC AND SOLICITING. THAT'S NOT ENOUGH?
NO!
NOBODY HERE HAS ENGAGED IN THAT!
OH YEAH? AND THIS...
...THIS ISN'T FOR YOUR FILM?
EXTRAS FOR A FILM SHOOT
XXX
FILM URGENT
$5 PER DAY
LOCK UP THE BARN AND ALL THEIR TRUCKS.
LEW...
I DIDN'T KNOW IT WAS ILLEGAL...I'M SORRY...
YOU'LL TELL THAT TO THE JUDGE!

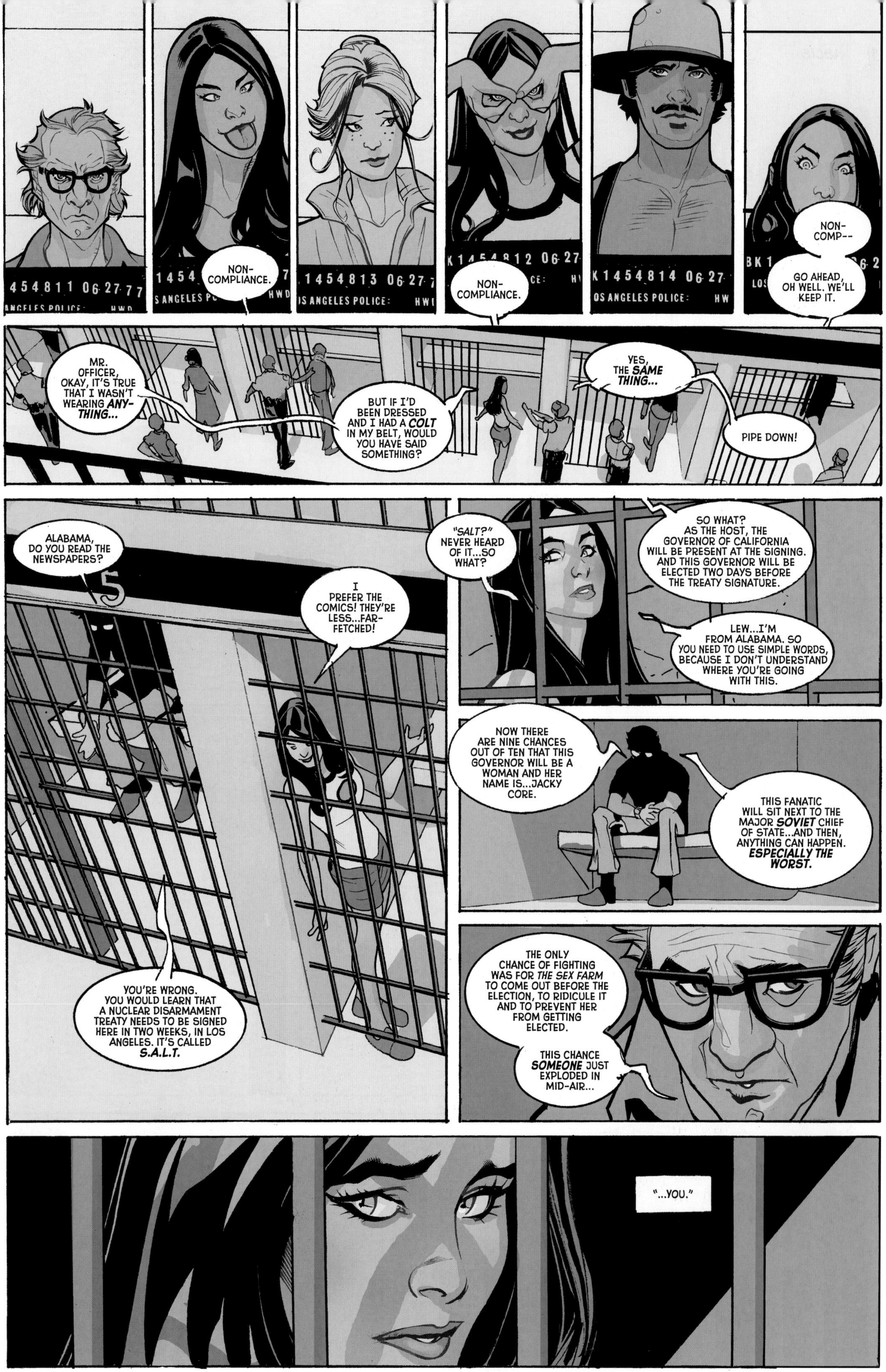
454811 06-27-77
ANGELES POLICE: HWD
1454 7
S ANGELES POLICE HWD
NON-COMPLIANCE.
1454813 06-27-7
LOS ANGELES POLICE: HWI
K 1454812 06-27-
NON-COMPLIANCE.
K 1454814 06-27-
LOS ANGELES POLICE: HW
NON-COMP--
GO AHEAD, OH WELL. WE'LL KEEP IT.
MR. OFFICER, OKAY, IT'S TRUE THAT I WASN'T WEARING ANYTHING...
BUT IF I'D BEEN DRESSED AND I HAD A COLT IN MY BELT, WOULD YOU HAVE SAID SOMETHING?
YES, THE SAME THING...
PIPE DOWN!
ALABAMA, DO YOU READ THE NEWSPAPERS?
I PREFER THE COMICS! THEY'RE LESS...FAR-FETCHED!
YOU'RE WRONG. YOU WOULD LEARN THAT A NUCLEAR DISARMAMENT TREATY NEEDS TO BE SIGNED HERE IN TWO WEEKS, IN LOS ANGELES. IT'S CALLED S.A.L.T.
"SALT?" NEVER HEARD OF IT...SO WHAT?
SO WHAT? AS THE HOST, THE GOVERNOR OF CALIFORNIA WILL BE PRESENT AT THE SIGNING. AND THIS GOVERNOR WILL BE ELECTED TWO DAYS BEFORE THE TREATY SIGNATURE.
LEW...I'M FROM ALABAMA. SO YOU NEED TO USE SIMPLE WORDS, BECAUSE I DON'T UNDERSTAND WHERE YOU'RE GOING WITH THIS.
NOW THERE ARE NINE CHANCES OUT OF TEN THAT THIS GOVERNOR WILL BE A WOMAN AND HER NAME IS...JACKY CORE.
THIS FANATIC WILL SIT NEXT TO THE MAJOR SOVIET CHIEF OF STATE...AND THEN, ANYTHING CAN HAPPEN. ESPECIALLY THE WORST.
THE ONLY CHANCE OF FIGHTING WAS FOR THE SEX FARM TO COME OUT BEFORE THE ELECTION, TO RIDICULE IT AND TO PREVENT HER FROM GETTING ELECTED.
THIS CHANCE SOMEONE JUST EXPLODED IN MID-AIR...
"...YOU."

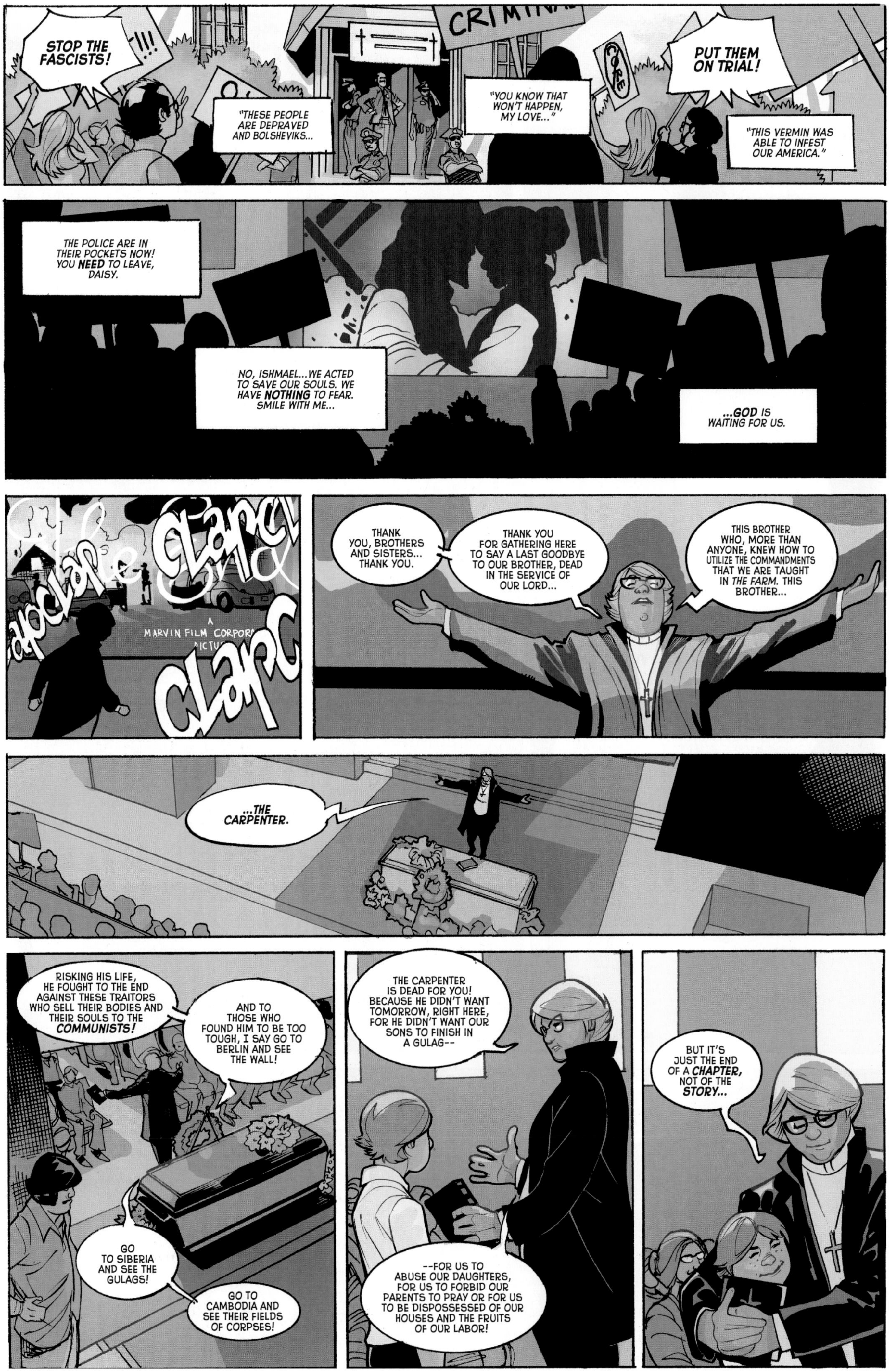
STOP THE FASCISTS!
!!!
CRIMIN
"THESE PEOPLE ARE DEPRAVED AND BOLSHEVIKS...
"YOU KNOW THAT WON'T HAPPEN, MY LOVE..."
PUT THEM ON TRIAL!
"THIS VERMIN WAS ABLE TO INFEST OUR AMERICA."
THE POLICE ARE IN THEIR POCKETS NOW! YOU NEED TO LEAVE, DAISY.
NO, ISHMAEL...WE ACTED TO SAVE OUR SOULS. WE HAVE NOTHING TO FEAR. SMILE WITH ME...
...GOD IS WAITING FOR US.
A MARVIN FILM CORPOR PICTU
CLAPC
THANK YOU, BROTHERS AND SISTERS... THANK YOU.
THANK YOU FOR GATHERING HERE TO SAY A LAST GOODBYE TO OUR BROTHER, DEAD IN THE SERVICE OF OUR LORD...
THIS BROTHER WHO, MORE THAN ANYONE, KNEW HOW TO UTILIZE THE COMMANDMENTS THAT WE ARE TAUGHT IN THE FARM. THIS BROTHER...
...THE CARPENTER.
RISKING HIS LIFE, HE FOUGHT TO THE END AGAINST THESE TRAITORS WHO SELL THEIR BODIES AND THEIR SOULS TO THE COMMUNISTS!
AND TO THOSE WHO FOUND HIM TO BE TOO TOUGH, I SAY GO TO BERLIN AND SEE THE WALL!
GO TO SIBERIA AND SEE THE GULAGS!
GO TO CAMBODIA AND SEE THEIR FIELDS OF CORPSES!
THE CARPENTER IS DEAD FOR YOU! BECAUSE HE DIDN'T WANT TOMORROW, RIGHT HERE, FOR HE DIDN'T WANT OUR SONS TO FINISH IN A GULAG--
--FOR US TO ABUSE OUR DAUGHTERS, FOR US TO FORBID OUR PARENTS TO PRAY OR FOR US TO BE DISPOSSESSED OF OUR HOUSES AND THE FRUITS OF OUR LABOR!
BUT IT'S JUST THE END OF A CHAPTER, NOT OF THE STORY...

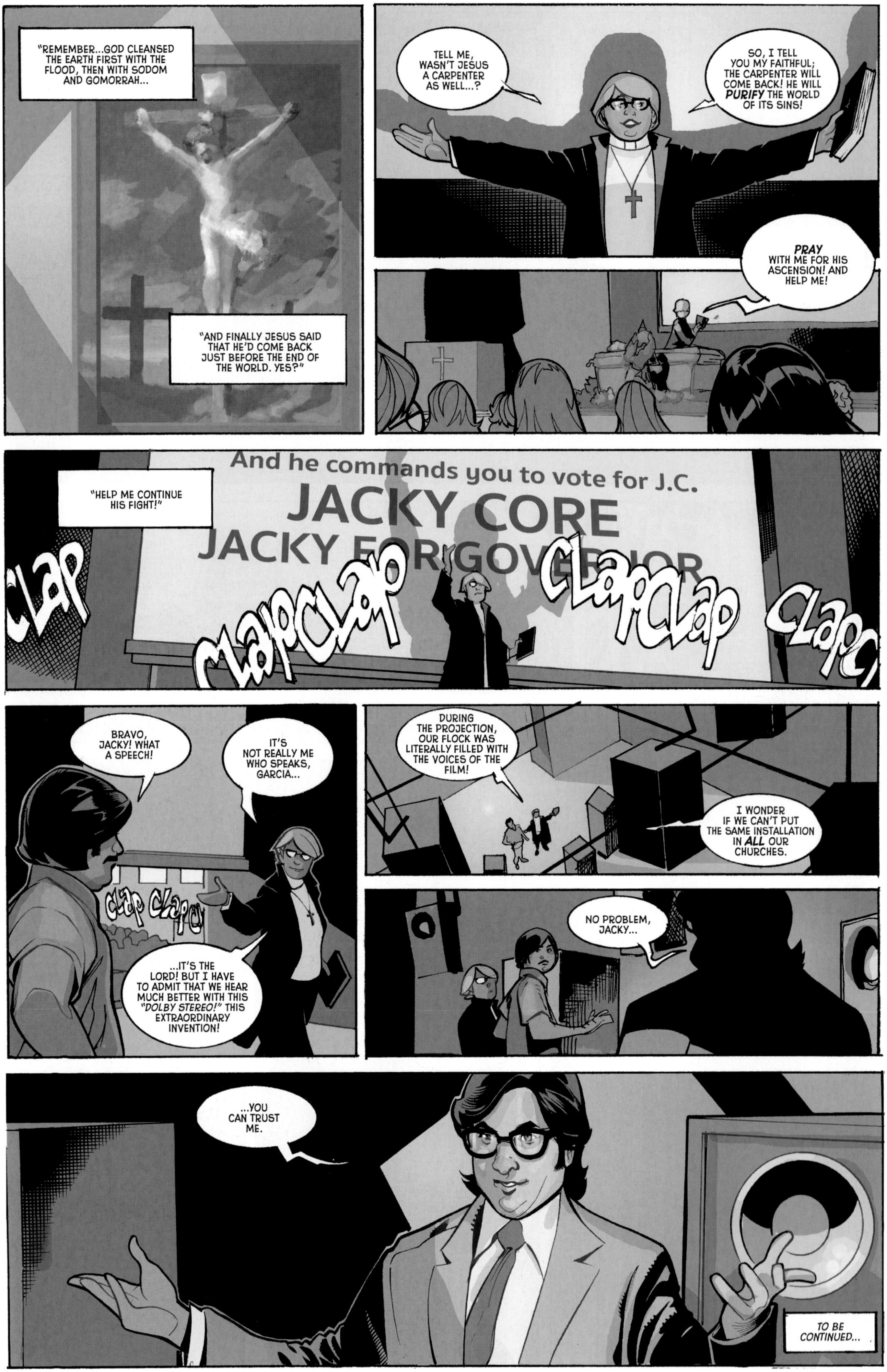
"REMEMBER...GOD CLEANSED THE EARTH FIRST WITH THE FLOOD, THEN WITH SODOM AND GOMORRAH...
"AND FINALLY JESUS SAID THAT HE'D COME BACK JUST BEFORE THE END OF THE WORLD. YES?"
TELL ME, WASN'T JESUS A CARPENTER AS WELL...?
SO, I TELL YOU MY FAITHFUL; THE CARPENTER WILL COME BACK! HE WILL PURIFY THE WORLD OF ITS SINS!
PRAY WITH ME FOR HIS ASCENSION! AND HELP ME!
"HELP ME CONTINUE HIS FIGHT!"
And he commands you to vote for J.C.
JACKY CORE
JACKY FOR GOVERNOR
CLAP
CLAPCLAP
CLAPCLAP
CLAPC
BRAVO, JACKY! WHAT A SPEECH!
IT'S NOT REALLY ME WHO SPEAKS, GARCIA...
CLAP CLAPCL
...IT'S THE LORD! BUT I HAVE TO ADMIT THAT WE HEAR MUCH BETTER WITH THIS "DOLBY STEREO!" THIS EXTRAORDINARY INVENTION!
DURING THE PROJECTION, OUR FLOCK WAS LITERALLY FILLED WITH THE VOICES OF THE FILM!
I WONDER IF WE CAN'T PUT THE SAME INSTALLATION IN ALL OUR CHURCHES.
NO PROBLEM, JACKY...
...YOU CAN TRUST ME.
TO BE CONTINUED...

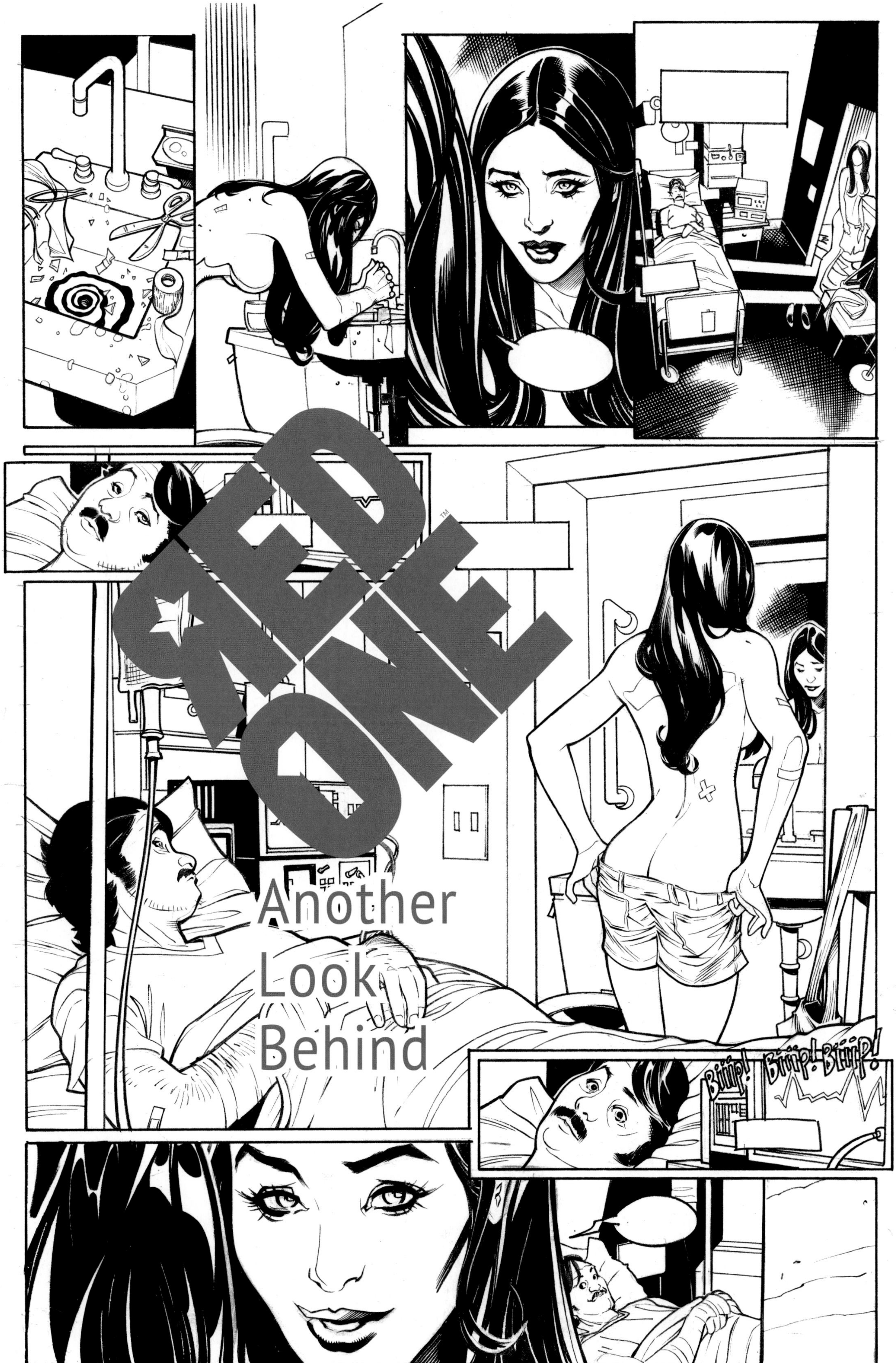
RED ONE
Another Look Behind
Biiip!
Biiiip!
Biiiip!

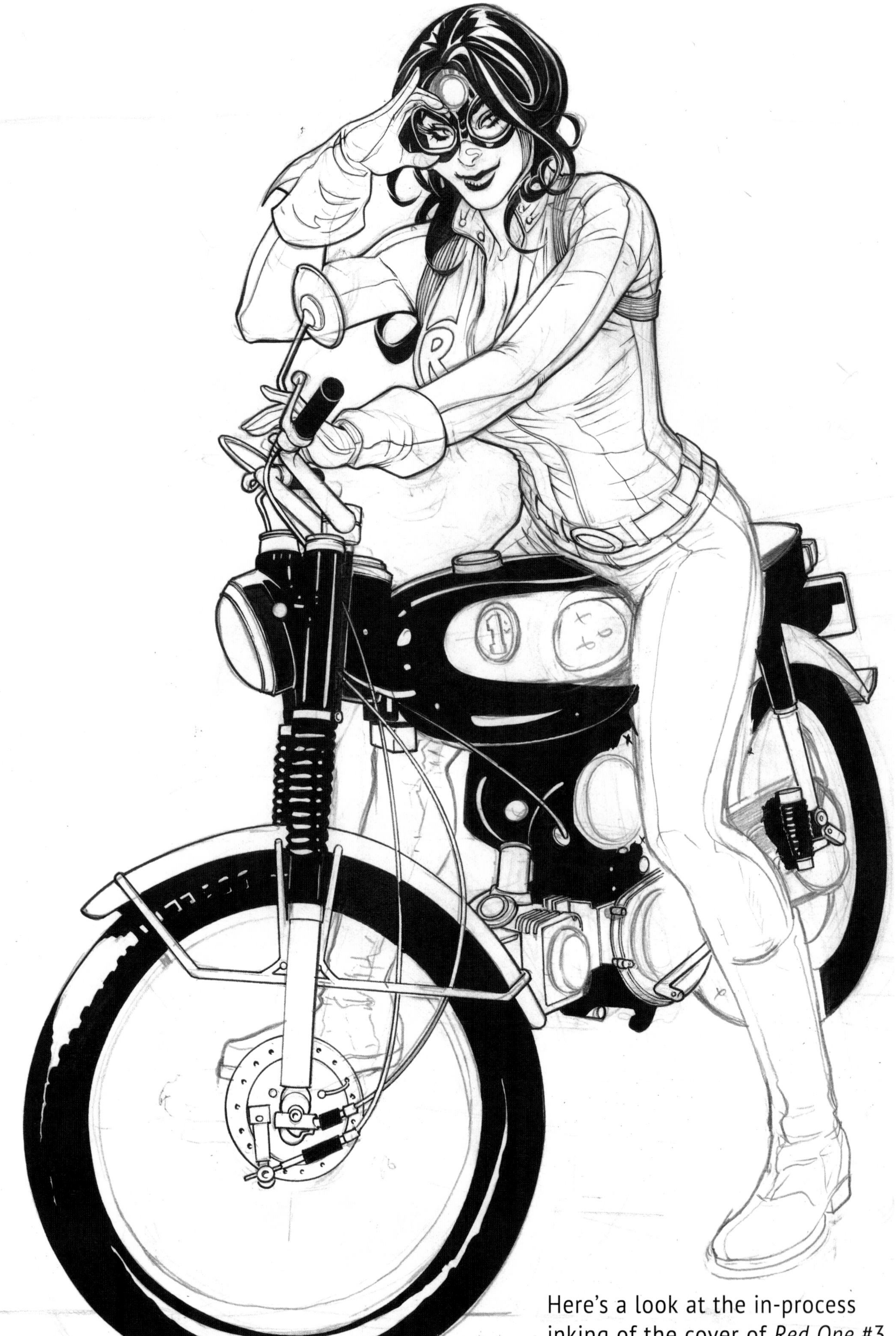

Here's a look at the in-process inking of the cover of *Red One* #3 by Rachel Dodson. Original art is 12" x 18" on Bristol board.

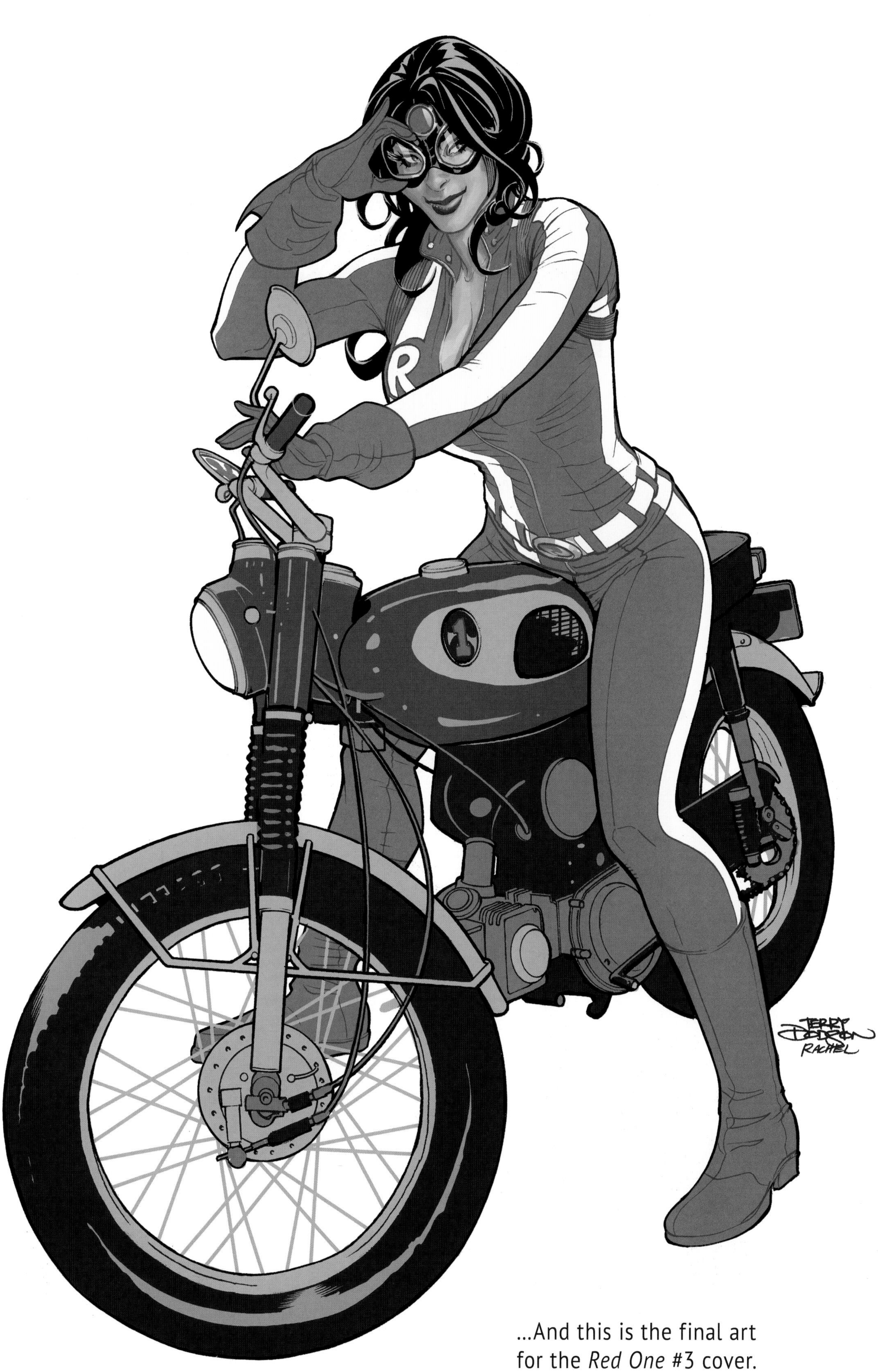
TERRY DODSON
RACHEL

...And this is the final art
for the *Red One* #3 cover.

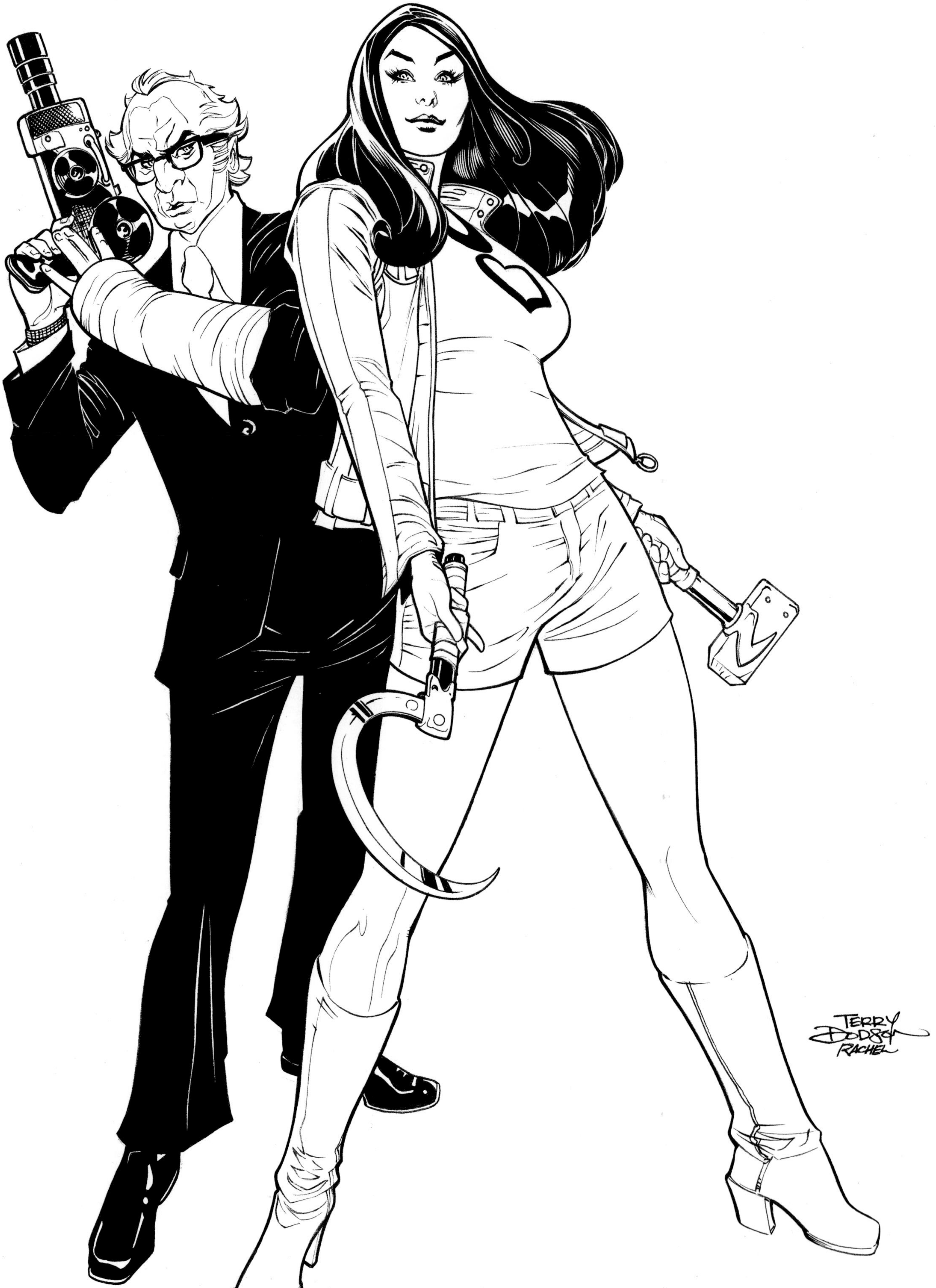
TERRY
DODSON
RACHEL

This is the final inked version of the *Red One* #4 cover by Rachel Dodson. Original art is 12” x 18” on Bristol board.

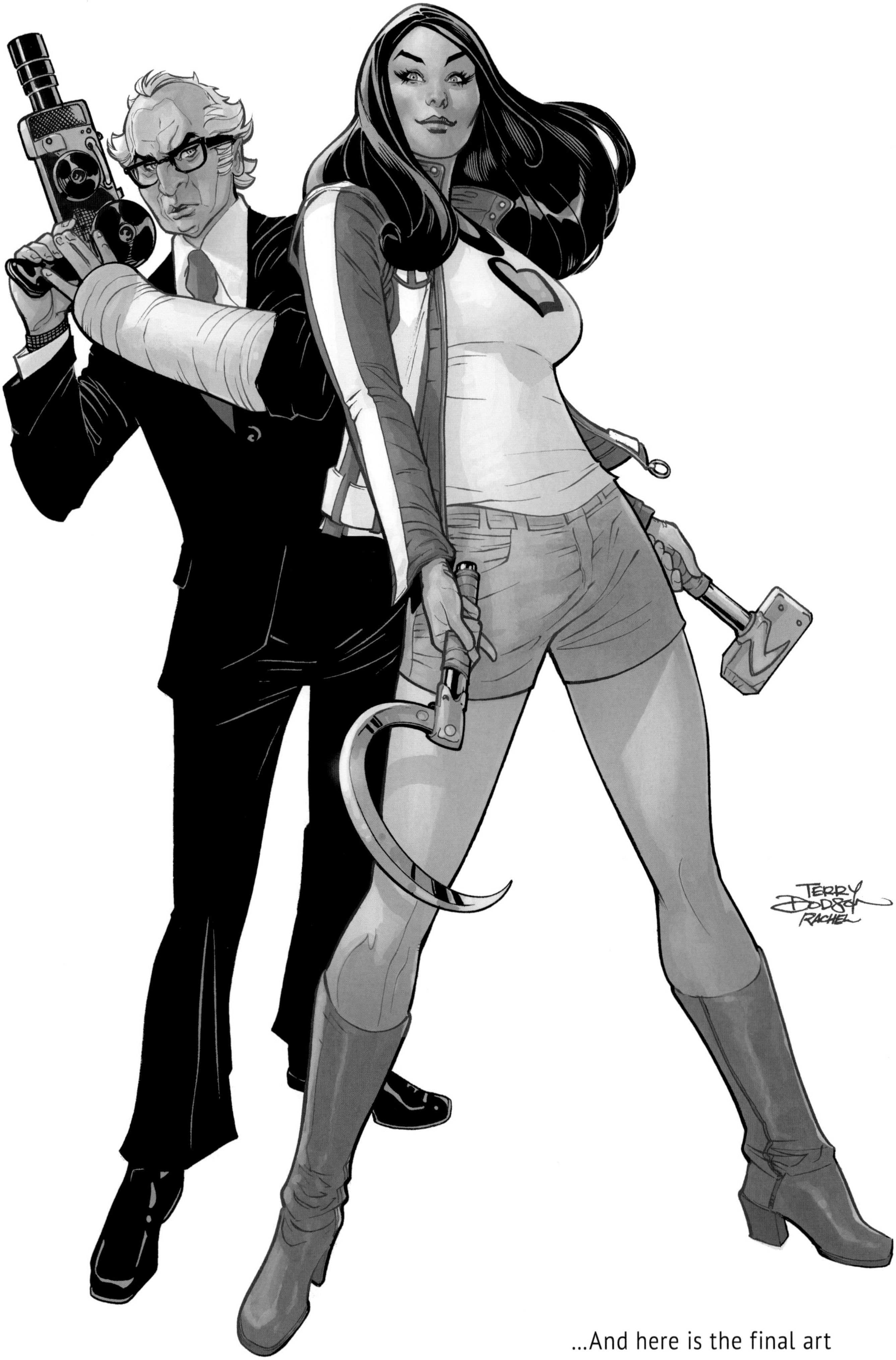
TERRY
DODSON
RACHEL

...And here is the final art
for the *Red One* #4 cover.

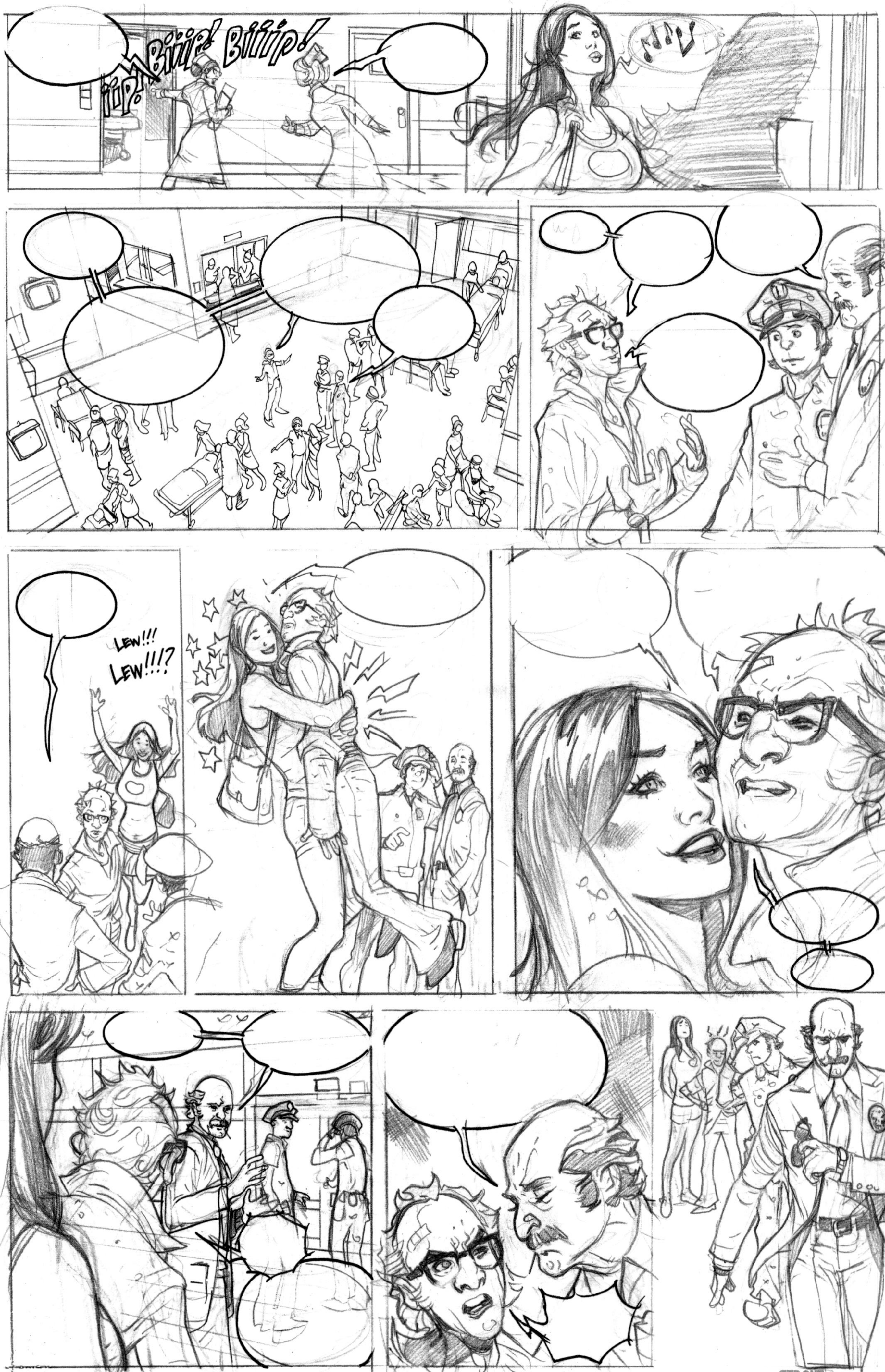
IIP! BIIIP! BIIIP!
LEW!!!
LEW!!!?
Terry's pencils for page 11.

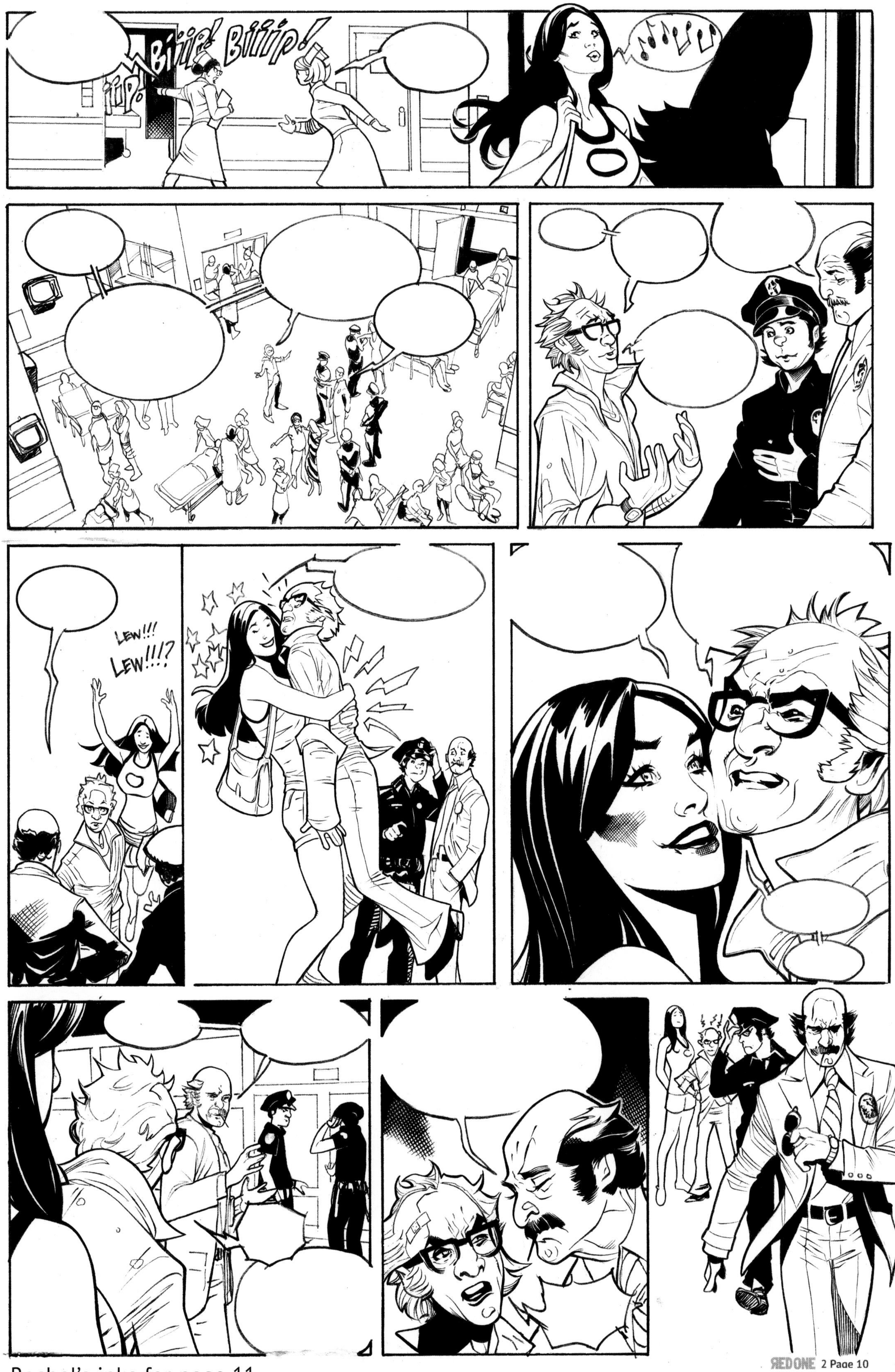
iip!
Biiip! Biiip!
LEW!!!
LEW!!!?

Rachel's inks for page 11.

TEAM RED ONE (L Terry Dodson, R Xavier Dorison) on a "research" trip.

TEAM RED ONE

Xavier Dorison writes in Paris.
Terry Dodson draws on the Oregon Coast.
Rachel Dodson rides horses.
Clayton Cowles bears with them.
Lauren Sankovitch abides.

Special thanks to Gillian Renk for the color flats, Philippe Hauri and
Editions Glénat for their continued support of the project, new Team Red One
member Lauren Sankovitch for her amazing editorial skills, to Eric Stephenson,
Jonathan Chan, and everyone at Image Comics, and, of course,
you, for your continued support of RED ONE!

www.redonecomic.com